OUTRIDING: THE OPEN LINE

OUTRIDING, Parts One through Four

BY JACOB CLIFTON

BREAKAWAY SOLDIER

OUTRIDING, PART I
BY JACOB CLIFTON

Chapter One: *The Rise & Spectacular Fall of One Empirical Empire*

Theodore Castelline kept to himself.

It wasn't a conscious decision, not really; it wasn't that he didn't like people. He loved them, in fact, though at a distance. If you'd asked him, in those days—back on the glorious City of Earth, jewel of the Commonwealth—he wouldn't really have known how to reply.

"I like to watch people," he'd say. "I like being of service."

Being of service was a big deal, in the Earth Alliance Defense Corporation from which he took his provenance. Most members of EADC would say the same, but the difference was that Theodore meant it. He liked fulfilling his duties, he liked going to bed exhausted. When it ended—and it ended with just a single word— he'd been a happy member of EADC for all his twenty-seven years.

His particular provenance was built on military conventions going back hundreds of years, to Earth's original constellation of government. EADC held its nationals in escrow until the age of eighteen, when they'd officially take oath and become a full citizen.

But for Theodore, it was never a decision: He knew he was EADC, just as his brothers and parents before him.

Nobody else put such an emphasis on service and style, at least in the brochures that came to his door on testing days: Of all the incorporated nations represented in large numbers on the City of Earth, EADC was the oldest and the nimblest. As childhood friends, coming up in their class of age, gradually sorted out into other companies, other nations, he never felt it was a loss: They'd made their choices, they could come back at any time. Belonging to another nation's flag wasn't the block to communication that it once had been, not with the Link.

At birth, all citizens—of any company—were fitted with an always-on connection that kept them tied to the nation of their choice. When defecting from one country to another, the process was as simple as application approval, transfer of shares, and reconnection to the hub of the nation of choice. Simple as a single word.

*

"Court Librarian, Orleans Regiment? Theodore Castelline?"

Theodore looked up from his desk, into the sunlight, squinting to see his visitor.

"Ted? Teddy?"

He shook his head, remembering to smile. He hoped it looked friendly.

"Theo, I guess. Never Ted."

Really, it was Theodore, but the man seemed nice enough. He stayed at attention until Theodore stood, arms bent back in military pose.

"Courier transfer. Are you currently engaged?"

"Nothing I can't do on the trip. Indexing a new data cache from a probe out past Saturn," he said excitedly, to nothing like a real response.

"Hard copies of a few executive orders, need hand-delivery. They sent me to you."

"They," in this case, most likely being the new Corporal in his division: A spitty, red-faced man who never seemed to comprehend the finer points of logic when he was feeling pressure. The kind of man who'd rather come to your office in person than simply open a screen, just to make sure you were at your desk—which were, of course, irrelevant, although Theodore liked sitting at his desk—or make snide remarks about your dress uniform, catch imaginary smudges on your shoes. A micromanager, who thought he was doing his job best when he was complaining, and sucked up just enough to his superiors to make this seem correct.

The Corporal loved sending Theodore on these pointless runs because he knew Theodore wouldn't complain, and he because he resented Theodore. Always imagining he was judging him, behind that blank helpful smile. Some people cannot look even into your eyes without just seeing themselves, and generally those people won't like what they see. There was no way, there were no words, that might disabuse him of that notion.

"Yes, sir. I see that you don't have the sense of a Pralthian stone-eater, sir, but I couldn't care less as long as you do your job, sir. And when you don't, I am more than happy to pick up the slack, sir."

Theodore didn't even like to think about saying something like that, it made him so nervous. You might as well ask for a one-way ticket to the Hades Nebula, or somewhere even worse, for insubordination like that. Even though Theodore wouldn't mean anything by it: The man *was* stupid, and crude, and *childish*, but none of that really mattered to Theodore one way or the other. The Corporal was just another hurdle to jump, on the stretch between waking up, and sitting at his desk, and doing his work until he was exhausted, and going back to bed again.

Theodore knew just enough about people to know they didn't want to hear that; everybody wants to be important, even if that means being a monster.

*

"You come up a Librarian, or transfer in? Never met one before."

Theodore spared a glance over at the visitor, who was setting quite a pace as they jogged through the complex. He imagined the guy had left the hardcopies in his own office by accident, but he didn't mind the exercise.

Since the Colonel, he'd felt chained down, afraid of a drop-by at any time. It was a lovely building if you wanted to stretch your legs: Long glass hallways, glass floors looking down on the Gulf, far below.

"Sir. From Basic. But we did the same training as everybody. You don't split off into the Sciences until twelfth. It was that or sniper, but I always wanted a desk job."

The man seemed surprised. He was a little bit older than Theodore, handsome in a way that would have intimidated his younger self. Since school he hadn't trusted the type: High back-and-sides, barrel chest. They seemed to get the meanest, if they didn't get their way.

"Sniper? Well hell, soldier, that was my first regiment. Got transferred into civil service when I got shot in the knee."

He pointed down, indicating his knee in case Theodore was unfamiliar.

"You saw action."

"Just a border skirmish. Back when they were still figuring out Uplift on the Barrows."

After its admittance into the galactic Union of governments, the Alliance on Earth had been pretty touchy about uplifting other planets and races. They'd come in with a bit of an upstart reputation, and marketing departments from twenty different firms had met to lay down the law: Don't do anything without galactic say-so. They're looking for a reason to knock you back down to the minors.

The second experiment in uplift, after Earth's centennial, had come about as an accident: Some miner with a major in Xenopsychology had skipped over some basic First Contact protocols, desperate to prove his worth and get transferred to research, which could have had a negligible effect but instead resulted in a disaster of near-planetary proportion, when the natives proved better at understanding nerve gas development than Earth itself. They weren't mean, but they weren't ready either; the Barrows Legions had paid the price.

"See one up close?"

Theodore didn't really care, and especially wasn't interested in hearing some hateful diatribe about aliens and Barrow shit-tossers, but there was something safe about the man's smile. Asking a man for anything, even a story, is the fastest way to make him like you. Theodore understood that too, although he never seemed to remember it when the time was right. When he tried to imagine getting close with the Colonel, fooling him somehow into thinking they weren't enemies, that was as close as Theodore ever got to angry. What a terrible thing that would be.

"Their heads are where your stomach would be. But hunker down close, their eyes look just the same as ours. More like deer than snakes, you get that jewel-refraction from far off makes 'em look like snakes, but close up they... You could see thinking, in there."

The man stayed quiet, heavy breaths echoing off the complex corridors as they jogged along.

"I couldn't really fight after that. You know how it ended?"

"Something about the nerve agents getting denatured, or..."

"That was the story, but it was a little more complicated than that. Or less complicated, maybe. Turned out they were just trying to take our poison, turn it back into something good. They didn't realize they were poisoning *us*—they just thought they were reversing our pollution. *For* us."

Theodore was amazed. Not what you'd expect from a front-liner.

"So how'd you get shot?"

He shook his head. Friendly fire?

"A family, refugee family. Way down deep in the catacombs. Didn't know the war was over, so they came out just gnashing at us. They grow to adult-sized real fast, you gotta look at the arms. The appendages. They don't grow claws for the first year. I didn't really think about it, just jumped in front of my sergeant to wave my hands around in his face, or something. Spooked him."

"And the family?"

"Got 'em above ground, all sorted. Turns out they were related to the main governing body, so we just brought 'em home and said sorry."

Theodore lingered in the doorway, once he'd gotten the hardcopy. Just couldn't seem to pull away. It seemed funny that such a thoughtful, nice guy would be stuck running around in his dress blues all day, working hours when a Link could do it instantly. Maybe he was just friendly.

Theodore didn't think the guy wanted him to leave, either. But he couldn't think of a thing to talk about, so he simply kicked the doorframe and asked dumb questions about the courier run.

"Yeah, you wanna take a tube down to Canaveral, and then I guess a conc to..."—he flicked his eyes up, and to the side, searching a menu—"...Conc periorbital gets you there in four hours, basically right to the training ground. They'll try to put you up for the night, but you don't want to get on their schedule or you'll have a hell of a day tomorrow—just turn right around and come back. Home by nine."

Theodore nodded. Nothing he couldn't have figured out for himself, just as instantly, but there was something nice about the gesture. Chivalrous, or... The man seemed to enjoy being of service, too.

"Born EADC?"

He nodded, with a proud grin.

"Going back to the beginning. One of my great-grands was US Army, back then."

Historically, nationality had been determined by the location of your birth. Money and religion weren't even part of it, for hundreds and hundreds of years: You just pledged allegiance to the flag they told you to, and stayed under it your whole life. It seemed crazy. But until humanity made the jump to the stars, no matter how technology advanced ahead of them, they couldn't seem to break with the idea that where you were mattered more than who.

"My family's from here, from the US Mid-Atlantic. Military, too."

"I didn't grow up on this side of the City. My mother was stationed in Australia the year I was born, a greening mission."

Theodore nodded appreciatively. Keeping and maintaining green spaces in the City of Earth was, for members of the EADC, one of the highest possible callings. It was embarrassing to talk about, though. EADC didn't like a tall poppy. The proudest positions tended to be the quietest.

"I had an aunt that worked in a vert farm. We used to go there in the summer."

"What campus?"

"Me? I attended here, mostly. I would remember you, I think."

"Yeah, I was on the Moon for most of school. Lottery. And then Basic I went to Chile, by request. I liked being on the beach, they've set up the whole thing so all you can see is coast, all the way down. Whole school."

"That sounds amazing. I've been to the ocean, but just when we were kids."

"Yeah, a buddy of mine turned me onto it just as I was graduating, or I wouldn't know. I guess people like to keep it a secret."

EADC liked to imply that every part of the City of Earth was equal, despite whatever landmasses history implied: The City stretched over the oceans, and up to the poles, so that everything was supposed to be equal in opportunity. But Theo had seen enough video to know that someplace like the Chilean coast probably needed to be downplayed in conversation. He liked that the guy told him about it.

"'Zat your wife?" he asked, falling into the soldier's rhythms. He liked the way he spoke.

The soldier cracked up.

"That's my sister from Basic! She's got two kids now."

Theodore nodded. He'd seen other people take on siblings and family throughout school that way, by affiliation, but never wanted to join up with another person's troubles. Marriage was one thing, but blood-brotherhood seemed like all the mess without the benefits.

"Ah, well. She's pretty."

"Took down a python for me, on Riverdale. Biggest sucker you ever saw. She wrestled it."

"Sounds like a good friend."

"Sister. She says hey, by the way. Heard us talking, on the Link."

"Hello, sister."

"Says you're pretty cute, too."

Theodore blushed, collecting his papers in a rush.

"Well, anyway. Thanks for the help, and the advice on travel. Is this where you usually office?"

"No, they've got me running ragged all day long. I'm home here, though. How about you?"

"I live about twenty blocks up from work, yeah. Short commute."

"What would you say to some coffee or something, when you're back from your trip?"

Theodore stumbled backward, as though tripping on something real and not just the slick carpet of the guy's office.

"I, uh... I don't actually know your name."

It wasn't an answer, but it was the honest truth.

"Listen, Theodore Castelline, Court Librarian. I'm not trying to make you uncomfortable..."

"—I would *like* to know it."

So the man—the Staff Sergeant Mick Caraghan—slipped him a card over Link, with his picture and everything, the full download. Vitals, hobbies, twenty favorite movies, a variety of pictures of him— mostly sunning himself—in various locales on- and off-world. Way more access than you'd have expected, if you were Theodore.

"I'll know when you're back in town, now. Don't be so shy, it's unbecoming of a decorated officer."

"I'll work on that. Sir."

Staff Sergeant Mick Caraghan laughed, and waved him out of his office.

"And don't let the Corporal get you down!"

Theodore nodded, laughing at himself a little bit. Even spared himself a little bit of a jig, heading back down. He didn't know, then, that it was the last time he'd ever see Mick Caraghan.

It was, in fact, one of the last things that ever happened to Theodore, in the Glorious City of Earth.

*

Perhaps it was Caraghan, then, that indirectly caused the trouble. Theo hadn't stumbled into something like that in a long time, and certainly not that sort of person. The kind of guy he'd have hated all schoolday, and dreamt of all night. It was a lot to process. Did Caraghan want children? Back up. Would Caraghan want to transfer his flag back to service, should something happen that required his services? Would they be snipers together, on some far-flung...

"Castelline. You've behind schedule."

The Corporal had opened a screen, for once. Theo smiled in a way he hoped was cringing and pathetic enough he'd be satisfied, but no luck. He could see red, creeping in up the neck.

"Corporal, I am, sir. I had to retrieve the hardcopies from the..."

"—I don't want excuses, Castelline, I want results. Those exec orders need to file by midnight their time, you hear me? It's high-level protocol changes, it can't be waiting around on your leave. Get yourself to the tube, soldier."

Four. They needed to be filed by *four* local. The guy never knew what he was talking about.

"Sir."

Once the screen clicked off Theodore rolled his eyes, but took care to monitor his breathing in case the Corporal was listening in. He'd gotten yelled at for that before, sighing and breathing or otherwise showing signs of life—once, for a particularly well-deserved razzberry—and didn't relish the thought of getting in any further with the dunce. Make him mad enough, he could do some real damage.

EADC didn't believe in sequestration or detention—on Link, the whole galaxy could be your jail—and so let its court-martialed citizens roam free. But without a vote, and without the power to transfer your flag or move shares until your stir was over, it was not a great life. They'd take care of your basic needs, of course—what else is a government for?—but entertainment and travel beyond your sector were shut down, and anybody with an EADC link could see exactly what was going on.

If things got real bad, or real personal, they could even transfer you to a new assignment. The boss two shuffles back—a mean-eyed drunk, who'd taken a shine to Theo for some unknown reason—had reassigned one of the louder guys in the office to three years of cleaner duty. Theo'd see him sometimes, in visits to the next sector over, mopping up and counting the days until he could come back to active military service. Doing a job that didn't need doing, just to cut the tall poppy down.

While defection could relieve you of those punitive duties, it couldn't release you from the tick-tock of your punishment—strict international rules about that—and so most countries marketed to those in stir with promises of easier punishments, reduced sentences and the like. But the cleaner fellow, for whom Theo'd never had much respect, wouldn't take a deal any more than Theo ever would.

If a man didn't stand by his corporation, what was he? Surely not a man. Better to take your lumps and get whatever experience you could out of it, than be known as a defector.

*

The conc was disgusting, as usual: A stomach-churning flip just out of the gravity well in a tin can the shape of a bullet, racked up with fifty other randoms, and then back again, locking into its landing zone with that magnetic buoyancy, like a slowly undulating nightmare trampoline.

To calm his nerves and rising gorge, Theodore clicked into a novel he'd heard some of the younger kids talking about: A ripped-from-the-news story about a guy who'd saved up his shares for thirty years, scuffling them off into side-accounts and hedge funds, until he was rich enough to declare himself a sovereign state. *The Empirical Empire*, he called it. *Its Rise and Spectacular Fall.*

Theodore couldn't concentrate on the story—too many sex scenes, breaking up the action—and he kept accidentally clicking it off, or louder, in his reverie. The eye control on his Link was a little loose, which generally he liked—his job meant keeping more screens open than your average data worker, and the slippery edges made for faster switching—but when it came to entertainment it could be really annoying. Rather than calibrating his screen to full, he switched off the video and just dreamed about his own little empire. Theodore Castelline Court Librarian, party of one. Maybe two.

*

Once he got to the training ground where the exec orders were to be delivered, and all the sentinels were laughing at him for coming all the way out when he could have emailed it with a glance, he lost the dreamy train of thought and settled his shoulders. Work.

Finally past the checks and into the high-grade offices, past the trainees and scut, Theodore took a moment to breathe. It was barely ten at night, so he was in under the wire, but considering four hours ago it had been the morning for him—he'd spent an hour, just this morning, with a flirty Staff Sergeant, a world away—he was feeling the pressure.

"Executive Orders? From Colonel Ashcleeve of the..."

"—Just set 'em on the pile, kid. We're in a hell of a cluster right now and I can't be updating protocols because one of you AE Central martinets has a hair up your ass about..."

"With respect, sir, I was told these needed to be filed by four? And I guess it's two local?"

"I don't give a good damn what you..."

"Sir. I only want to make sure I've followed the proper procedure. I don't mean to add pressure. In fact, is there anything I can do? Including silently walk out of here?"

The Lieutenant—twice Theo's age, balding into a tonsure, mustache bristled just within regulation—looked up at him, squinting.

"Sure doesn't sound like any EA geek I've ever met. Come over here."

The Lieutenant moved his banker's light out of the way to focus on Theodore.

"You've gotta be kidding me. They send me some kind of kid... Listen, what is your post? You a Media guy? Marketing, maybe? You look clean, like that."

"Library Clerk, sir. Occasional courier to the, um, to Colonel..."

"Oh, I'm familiar with him, kid. Sorry I barked."

"Urgency. We all have a different definition for urgency, sir. Some more flexible than others."

"You've got a way with words, kid. Almost sounds like you're not being completely insubordinate."

"We at the AEDC Central Office take insubordination and other protocol violations very seriously, sir."

The old man laughed, and slapped his knee. He pulled a flask from a desk drawer—real wood, maybe a museum piece even—and shoved a pile of papers aside to pour out a couple of tumblers.

"What's the career tree for somebody like you? Lots of room upwards?"

"They say so, sir. But in practice... They shuffle 'em around, up higher than me, and we don't get a lot of opportunity to advance. Plus Library, it's not... The number of things not in Link never goes up. I mostly just assimilate the news, dev reports. Things that are happening. Everything that can be catalogued already has, so there aren't any special projects, or..."

"I had a girl once, Library. She said the same thing. Her dream was to find some kind of cache or forgotten probe and spend her life just working out the edges. Everything for everyone."

Theo nodded. It was the kind of sentiment that had made his eyes tear up, in Basic. Everything for everyone. All data, everywhere, seamlessly discoverable as quickly as you needed it. The Librarian's Grail. The only people he could trust, when he was coming up, were the kind of people who understood that. This Lieutenant was an unlikely ally.

"So we just get our new boss every year or so, and teach him the way we do things, and then he gets his promotion or takes a lateral position because he's bored, and it's the next guy. I'm good at my job, though, and proud of that. I don't mind..."

The old fellow cocked an eyebrow.

"Sir, I *don't* mind. That's not the company line, it's the literal truth. Never much cared for management."

"Said a mouthful there, kid."

The Lieutenant clinked the glasses, leaving Theodore's on the desk. A wet circle remained behind his: They were real glass.

"I mean, I wouldn't care to be in management, of course. You learn something new from everybody that orders you around. Even..."

He grinned, urging Theodore on with his shoulders.

"From everybody. It's a good life. I live twenty blocks up from my office..."

"—They've still got you all in offices? I had to bite and claw people's faces to get this desk. You don't seem like the type."

"I can desk anywhere. But I like having a place to go."

"And he likes having a place to come and find you."

The man broke out laughing again, at Theo's chagrin. He really did seem to have the Colonel's number.

"What about you, a lateral move? Can't you transfer out from under? See a little of the world."

Maybe once upon a time. But now when he thought about that, he just got tired.

"EA Central, sir. I'm where the action is. At least, my kind of action. He's not the only thing keeping me there."

And as of this morning, he wasn't even in the top five. Perhaps seeing the momentary lapse in focus that today's little adventure brought on, the old man nudged his glass again. Exactly the sort of thing that stressed Theodore out the most: It was only noon for him, local, which meant he'd be drinking in the morning—subjectively— but also on the job. It would make the conc back home even worse. But then, he didn't want to be rude. Maybe he could nap, flying back?

"Well, consider this. Next time that little shit spits in your eye, with his red pug face, you just consider this. We got a good outfit, out here. Nobody throws their weight around. We know the difference between the spirit and the letter. Now, I'm not asking you to come work for me—I like your style, but I don't need a Librarian—but I'm telling you, there are more crews like ours than there are of his."

"I... Appreciate the sentiment, sir. More than you know."

Theodore took the drink and downed it, not wanting to be rude.

"And I do know what you're talking about. I wouldn't be EADC if I didn't believe it. If this was all I knew, or this man's behavior were the most important thing, I would defect out in a second. You have me there. But I have responsibilities, I have people..."

"I thought I detected a little something in there. You got yourself a girl?"

"A guy. Maybe. Maybe something. As of four hours ago."

"And you tore yourself away from that, for this? To bring me this shit?"

"He was the one that handed off the assignment, sir. And I don't even know..."

"Listen, kid. You go home. You freshen up and you see where that heads. I'm your elder, and I'm smarter than you, and I know how quickly these things move."

"Sir. Yes, sir."

Theodore thought about trading cards with the old buzzard, even imagined coming back here on a leave if he ever got one... And then his eyes fell on the pile of paperwork he'd shoved over, so near the edge of the desk.

"Sir, is that the..."

They both looked down at the hardcopy. What should have read, brightly emblazoned with the EADC logo, "EXEC ORDER #483209," instead said simply, *Allied Effects Monthly*. A car-accessories catalog.

"Well, I'll be. You came six time zones across the world to bring me a toy catalog? I don't even drive, kid."

Well. The vodka started doing tricks. And didn't stop until... Well, it never stopped.

*

"You know how much goddamn money and time you wasted on this little errand?"

"Sir, yes sir."

"And you understand that those protocols aren't locked in now until the next cycle? Another waste of a fortune?"

"Sir, I've already emailed the Lieutenant with the correct paperwork, and shipped him hardcopies, while I was on the conc back. I checked in with the heads of three departments and they've all assured me that there is no diff..."

"—I don't give a... You little clerk, I gave you an order!"

"Yes, sir, which I fulfilled to the best of my ability. I'm afraid I didn't double-check the..."

"Are you blaming my Staff Sergeant for this little mix-up? Why don't we Link him right now, you can say that to his face. Or better yet, I can call him into the office and you can dress him down in person."

"Sir, no sir. That won't be necessary, sir. I take full responsibility."

"That's right, you do."

"Sir, I am willing to do whatever I can to..."

"—I don't need the sniveling, Librarian. I don't need it. I know what you think of me, I don't need the whole song and dance."

"With respect, sir, I would merely like to state, again, that I am willing to take on whatever extra work or sacrifice is necessary to..."

"—I don't want your extra work, or your goddamned sacrifice! I want goddamn excellence."

Theo sat with his hands in his lap, coming close to being sick all over the old geezer. It was one thing to be called to the carpet, or threatened with embarrassment in front of Caraghan. Quite another to get reamed for no reason, in a classic Colonel zero-sum situation like this. With no options, he sat quietly, wondering what response would get this over with the fastest.

"Nothing to say? Thought so. I've been looking at your jacket, you know. Sniper skills excellent, it says. Fit for duty, it says. Have to wonder to myself exactly what it was got you sent down here to the stacks, where I have to look at your stupid face every day."

You don't, is the thing. You dumb old shit. You don't have to do any of this. The world is better than that, it anticipates your needs, it performs efficiently, and you can't even see it. This whole thing is one big party for you, your ego, your broken down old limp...

"Eyes on mine when I'm talking to you, you insubordinate little..."

"Sir, like all meetings, this is being recorded."

"Yeah, and what's your point?"

"If you're going to report me upstairs, I'd appreciate it if you'd cut to the chase. If you're going to let me go with a warning, or a punishment, please do issue it. If you'd like to see me transferred, let's talk about that. But I am too tired right now to do anything else. I can't listen to this. I don't want to show you any disrespect..."

"—You don't wanna show me any..."

"—But I'm not sure I'll have the option much longer. You're being abusive, and your behavior is unbecoming to an officer of the EADC. I understand your disappointment and I share it. I wish I could have gotten this one right, because instead I have wasted an entire day of work. Work, sir, on my actual job. I am now behind on my own duties, because I took a day off, because you requested it."

"I won't be spoken to this way, Court Librarian. I'll shove you so far out into space they'll be looking for your junk trail..."

"—Again, sir. This meeting is being recorded. I have answered your questions, apologized for my mistake, and wish to give you no further problems."

"Your further problems just started, you little shit. You've wasted my time, you've wasted our company's time, you've embarrassed us all, and don't think we didn't take note of your little trip to the Sergeant's office—which, by the way, could easily fall under fraternization protocol if I decide."

"You... You're threatening to ground me from seeing other soldiers socially? Outside my duties?"

"That is only the beginning of what I am threatening to do."

Theodore stood.

"Then you can go fuck yourself, sir."

And those were the last words Theodore Castelline ever spoke, in the City of Earth.

Chapter Two: *Carrier's Outriding*

The man that met Theodore Castelline at Processing was tiny. And *scary*.

His nametag read BOBBY GREENER, and his hair spiked right up in the air. It didn't seem silly, or over-fashioned, though: It seemed like a natural warning, like a rattlesnake's rattle. He carried a tablet—an anachronistic touch Theodore liked—and carried an earpiece over one ear.

"Theodore Castelline, Court Librarian. Will you be transferring your flag?"

Theo shook his head, confused. He hadn't been tossed out of Earth Alliance Defense Corp., or stripped of any honors. Terminating an employee's contract was a hugely newsworthy move, and after his career-ending "personal attack" on a commanding officer they just wanted him gone. So they'd sent him here, to Carrier's Outriding, to oversee the archival procedures for the ship's 100,000-year history: Essentially, a death sentence.

"I didn't think that was the deal. I'm EADC, we don't..."

"It's fine, I just wanted to know. You transfer 49% of your shares to Outriding Ltd. And you'll have most of the perks of dual citizenship."

Just not a vote or a say, he understood, nodding: Room and board, like any other contract, but without the feeling of being home or connected to anybody via Link. Still. It's not like anybody back home would be talking to him, any time soon. He couldn't face his family, and his only real friend was someone he'd just met the day he got sent up.

"I can do that. I mean, whatever gets me on your Link hub. I've been blind since I..."

The little man held up his hand. He couldn't be more than twenty-two, but his will was clearly implacable.

"Already taken care of. I'll show you the map..."

Bobby opened a screen before them, and showed him home.

*

"The average citizen of the system probably thinks of Outriding as some kind of Wild West fantasy, like a depot for cattle rustlers. And it's true, we get a fair share of undesirables coming through. But we have a stable population of over four billion, from all over the known universe, so we're a pretty rich keystone for of culture. Marketplace, diplomatic free space..."

He brought up the body of the thing, as seen from the outside: Six interlocking rings, each swinging freely, attached at two hinges. In her middle, open space for the port, and you could see them, a motley collection of every kind of ship and vessel. Theodore was in cryo when they docked, so he hadn't gotten to see it, but he imagined it was a sight: All those lives and machines, floating protected while the rings swung around in their graceful, strange arcs.

"But that's nothing, especially not to you. Carrier's Outriding is a living Alexandria, built for unknown purpose by unknown parties, maybe hundreds of thousands of years ago. The repository of every bit of knowledge and information radiation she's been able to collect in all that time. The secrets of life in this universe, maybe. Maybe just a lot of crap. That's what you're here to help figure out."

Bobby Greener spared him a quick up and down, with an eyebrow raised.

"...You come, uh, highly recommended."

He pointed at various spots on the rings, lighting them up faster than a child's game of Simon, rattling them off. Theodore knew he wasn't really trying to be rude: All this data was available, Greener was just bringing it to life.

"Valet, Security & Defense Services are performed by the Mockingbird Squad. You've probably heard of them..."

Theodore had, but only dirty stuff. They were ageless clones, men and women of perfected physicality, spliced with the traits of a million intergalactic races. All the movies and TV shows painted them as unspeaking, sometimes terrifying bodyguard sex robots, but in interviews they just seemed like basic, normal military. He'd never doubted they'd get along.

"This is their place, the Aerie. It's one of the only living spaces on the entire outer rim, you don't wanna go there. Most people get sick. Gravity goes..."

Bobby Greener shuddered. Theodore was delighted by even this simple sign of humanity.

"It's *bad*. Okay, and then over here we have Command, all along the center Ring. You'll be dealing with Chiefs of Staff, if you ever even see them, but at the top of the chain is Captain Bellar. Everybody answers to her, including the diplomats. And the Mockingbirds."

Her face popped up: A white scar down her dark skin, eyepatch like a pirate queen. Her glossy black hair cascaded down her back, and the marketing headshot showed her in "gal with a gun" mode: Straight-backed, gun up, looking down her taut shoulder at the camera. *Staring* it down, in fact. Theodore suppressed a shudder of his own, which he could tell irritated Bobby Greener.

"She's the Captain. You haven't seen military discipline until you meet a merc from the old guilds. I don't think the woman sleeps. She'd do anything for her people. That includes *you*."

"—*Just don't get on her bad side*! Isn't that right, Green?"

"Gree*ner*," Bobby Greener corrected automatically, squinting at the sudden painful slap on his back from the giant interrupting them. He stuck out one huge meaty hand, squeezing Theodore's until he thought it would pop, pumping it up and down.

"Bryce Dexter, Captain's Second!"

Theodore knew him from their corporate propo, but it was still something to see him in real life: The public face of Outriding. Bryce Dexter had his own action figures back home. To all appearances a preening, silly megalomaniac, he was still beloved across human space: A former pulp hero, a superman among men. *"He's seen every planet and gotten into scrapes with more races than you've ever seen!"* went the catchphrase, but it was basically true: He'd seen action all along the Rim, even been on some of the best exploratory missions of the recent decades.

One video, in fact, Theodore had very much enjoyed: The time Bryce Dexter piloted a bullet shuttle down past one gas giant's moon's deadly electric storms for an emergency landing, nailed it, and then turned the camera back on himself. Something about the man's cleft-chinned, lantern-jawed affect—usually so annoying to Theodore, who couldn't gain weight to save his life—was outmatched by the excitement and pride in his slightly wild eyes.

The glee there was charming, there was no denying it. It turned him from blandly handsome to something a bit more interesting, a little more inviting. He threw back his head in the video, turning off the camera as he did so, so the last image you'd see once the file was done was just him, collapsing back in hysterical laughter at another victory.

In real life, though, his eyes were sad. Still wild, but a little sad.

"You're the new clerk, right? The librarian! I haven't been to Earth in a dog's age. Keeping it clean?"

Theodore could do little more than nod, annoyed to think Dexter probably pegged him for starstruck, but somehow unable to do anything that didn't contribute to that illusion. Maybe, just a little, he was.

He remembered to remove his hand from the man's gigantic paws, and turned back to Bobby Greener, whose irritation was eloquent and chilling.

"I was just giving Theodore the tour, Officer Dexter. If you wouldn't mind..."

Bryce Dexter ducked his head, in a *very* off-message sign of embarrassment, and crinkled those kindly eyes back at Theo, nodding.

"Apologies, Mr. Greener. I'll let you get back to it."

He didn't run, but he stomped away quickly enough Theo could feel it through the floor.

*

"*Anyway*," Bobby Greener said darkly, and turned back to the screen.

"That's Dexter's office there. He's not so bad, just... You only have so many minutes to get a job done, whatever it is, and if he's in half a ring's radius it just seems to take twice as long. Automatically. He's like a fish in an aquarium. Infinitely expanding..."

Theodore nodded, in what he hoped was a friendly way, and Bobby snapped back into himself.

"Okay, now down here in the middle rims are Lorna and Shen. Lorna Sciorro is the Head Engineer, she runs the Machine Team. Shenayla B'Coreneis is the station's Systems Manager, so you'll be seeing more of her. They work together: Outriding is a living being. They like to say they take care of her body and her mind, respectively."

If anyone was likely to quiz you at the end of this rushed orientation, Bobby Greener seemed like the type. But Theodore was willing to go along with the ride, and memorize enough details later so he'd recognize the people when he met them in person.

"Lorna's cool. She knows more about Outriding's twists and turns and spatial anomalies than anyone alive. Her life's work is her life's study: Outriding's metals and compounds, the way she balances our ecosystem..."

Lorna was a laughing, solid woman in overalls; Theodore liked her immediately. The other one seemed cold, and strange. He looked more closely for a second, and when he finally remembered her,

Greener nodded. Yes, *that* Shenayla B'Coreneis. Famous anarchist; feral child-turned-pop icon.

"Our very own Valentine Tarzan Smith. She's pretty much the same kid, just grown up. I wouldn't mess with her. Keeping her happy is a huge part of your job, I'm going to be honest. She holds the keys to the kingdom—you're just a vassal. As far as they're concerned, you're a tool she's using. She doesn't really care about the data itself, so much as the *structure* of the data. Very protective of our girl..."

Theodore couldn't imagine what he would ever say to the woman, but it sounded like they'd be working together. He hoped she wasn't as terrible as she seemed. He had loved her wildness, growing up, watching them chase her all over Sol system, but she didn't seem to leave a lot of room to be gracious. When he thought of her, what her company had done to her back then, it made him feel guilty for loving AEDC so much. Or naïve.

"Like I don't really have time for you today? I'm not trying to—that was rude—but it's just we've got three different delegations coming in, and two of them are mutually kill-on-sight enemies, and I have to... You know I'm usually the VIP liaison, right? Have you seen, did you watch any of the prep videos on your way up?"

No, honestly. Even with the slips in and out of cryo during FTL, he'd still spent a subjective week on the liner, padding around in stocking feet, unable to get regular REM no matter how much he drank. He'd always found Outriding interesting, but in the way you wonder what it would feel like to touch a boa constrictor, or take a bullet in the arm. Never something that happens to *you*.

And so when they'd taken him and his knapsack of crap and put him on the liner—which was, he was made to understand, fairly more luxurious than he deserved—the last thing he'd wanted to do was read all about it. The fantastic cell he'd be locked in for the rest of his life.

"Well, you should. You're going to be a public face too, now. You're a Staff Chief. The fact you don't have any direct reports doesn't change that. You should get it together on deportment and clothes and stuff. Which, speaking of, I'm going to hand you off to our Protocol Director, who I see is on his way. Don't be frightened of him. He looks like hell."

*

Karnides—"Just Karnides, thanks"—didn't really look like *hell*, but he did look like a bit of bad mess.

Muttonchop sideburns and a black pompadour, scars down both his cheeks that didn't look ornamental, and just one biological arm— everything was a choice. You could get vat skin, vat limbs. *This is just a costume he wears*, Theodore thought. *Probably a pussycat under all the...*

"—Let's move," the guy growled on approach, taking his arm, and a quickly receding Bobby Greener shrugged as Theodore looked back, over his shoulder. He waved goodbye, taken up in Karnides's hurry, and immediately felt silly about that. It wasn't like they'd be friends. But Bobby waved back distractedly, already back issuing orders over his silly earpiece.

"I have my job because I love it, and because Bellar trusts me. I take comfort in the administration and elucidation of intercorporate etiquette and diplomacy. I like it when things go nicely. I like good *behavior*. Do you understand? I like things to go *smooth*."

"I'm sorry, I've been on a liner for a week and didn't sleep before that, so I might not be taking all of this in..."

Karnides walked with a sullen, sloping gait. His hairy, thick arms swung down low, like a gorilla, and he scowled as he went. Theodore couldn't figure out how he was moving so fast.

"You don't worry about that, Castelline. You worry about staying on the move until we get you settled. New faces attract attention, and you do not want attention. If anybody bothers you, you come straight to me. The Mockingbirds are great, but they come in flocks. Sometimes you need immediate help. And I don't care if you can't remember my name, or where my office is. That's Bobby's tune. He plays it well. But the rest of us, we won't say anything if you open up a private screen to remind you who we are. Everybody does that. Frankly it's good to be shown paying attention. So you just keep your eyes open."

Karnides ushered him swiftly onto one of the shuttle tubes that lined the inside and outside of each of Outriding's rings—an experience Theodore had been dreading—and once he'd shooed everyone else out of the car—"Station business, take the next one"—he looked at Theodore expectantly. Theodore cleared his throat.

"Do you... Like questions? Can I ask you questions?"

The beast shrugged, eyes glinting.

"Won't know anything otherwise."

"What is your actual *job*?"

"Before anybody comes to the Station we have a little warning. I use that time—and your information—to put together a dossier on how we do things. When they take their tea, or, Don't look in their right eye, Don't use certain words or their cognates, Talk to the eldest female first or nod or bow or curtsey. Who's allowed to deal with them, who *isn't*. I send out these reports, you read them. I keep tabs on where they're going, and work with Bobby and the Teams to curate their experience. We get a lot of types, here. They have to fit together. I do that. And when I fail..."

Karnides crushed one fist into the other, with a hairy steel crack.

"So I don't fail. I'm tight with the stable population, different factions and stuff, so they don't give me trouble. Tough customers, some of them. You gotta be pretty angry to chase your tail all the way to the ass-end of known space. *Don't* get mixed up with them. And if anybody approaches you that's not on Staff—even if they're friendly—I want a heads up. Protocol. You're not sequestered or anything, I just want you safe. Got me?"

With one thick hand on his back, Karnides guided Theodore out of the shuttle—whose movement hadn't even registered, to great relief—and out into the Hinge: One of two large spherical spaces that held the swinging rings together.

"One more Ring in—follow the red line—and then your screen can get you to Salter's office. She's your reporting manager, Communications Director. It's a small department, so you'll get to know her and Megan real well."

Karnides stopped himself, suddenly, drawing up to a surprising height. Nodding once, never breaking eye contact, he stuck out his right hand.

"Theodore, it has been a pleasure to meet you and to welcome you to Carrier's Outriding. She's a good ship, with a good heart, and we're a good crew. I know we look like a bunch of misfits, but we are okay. I will check on you in the coming days, so I want you to have a list ready of anything at all that would make your life comfortable. Make it *good*. I know this isn't a return trip, and you will consider it *my* job to make up for that."

He lowered his head, to look into Theodore's eyes.

"You were treated badly. I won't let that happen again."

Karnides clicked his heels—was this part of the Castelline dossier, this formal military stuff?—and was gone, Theodore staring after.

If this was how the guy treated fussy little strangers, how did he treat his friends? Did he *have* friends? Did everybody adore him as much as Theodore suddenly did? And most important of all: Was he some sort of lycanthrope? Did those *exist*?

Theodore laughed, across the Hinge toward the other tube: What a *comforting* werewolf Karnides would make.

*

Theodore was so stuck on the notion that he couldn't really take in all the aliens and people and smells and sounds of the Hinge. It felt like an open-air market, half public square and half bazaar. In a hundred years he'd never get to know a tenth of these people, who they were or even *what* they were. Where they came from, what their languages sounded like. He wondered if the other Hinge were the same.

His head was turned enough, in fact, that he missed out on a few central clues that would have cleared up the next two hellish days:

One woman, weeping, covered in tattoos that ran down her face to her arms in a pattern he recognized vaguely as being from around Scorpio, maybe, cried out against her Gods, while women—her sisters?—tried to comfort her.

"He was so close to death," the woman wept. "We could have had moments."

"He is with the Elders now, Sheghal. Mourn him not."

"It could have been so peaceful. He was at peace. I was nearly at peace. I lost him from the Link, couldn't feel him in my head, and then this fire. It could have been peaceful."

"He went, Sheghal. It is not ours to..."

"—He went up like a match's head, Kolev. Brimstone and fire, in our lover's bed. That's not the Gods. That's a terror. You'll see. By my light I see it, with an eye. Fire."

Another group several stalls away nodded, their tentacles waving slowly. One raised a hand out to her, evangelical, while the others hissed a calming susurrus.

"It comes too. It was an hour ago, this these. One hour, not more. It came, fire. As you say. First the head, then the body, then the mind. Sulfuric. We lost him, and with him a dream. Our dreams are less. He was at the edge of death. We are cast out, all. An hour ago. These, this."

The woman, weeping, stepped with painted arms outstretched, questioningly, and the alien reached for her in turn. He clasped her to him, in a mourner's embrace, and they wept quietly together while their people looked on, nodding sadly.

Theo took it in—no way of knowing these two groups of pilgrims had nursed a bitter enmity for the last six weeks, spitting at each other's stalls, issuing pejoratives in stage whispers—but he didn't really listen, or notice.

He just saw an exotic woman, hugging a crazy-looking alien, and thought, *How nice*. And then back to shaking his head, giggling about his werewolf.

*

Megan Quire intercepted Theodore on his way to Salter's office, which turned out to be a blessing in disguise. She was a font of knowledge on—well, lots of things generally—but their boss specifically. Her manic russet curls bounced around as she spoke, waving arms madly, in a plain white shift that showed off her ruddy brown skin and bright Irish features.

"Chief of Sociology. Or I mean, inclusively 'sociology,' as understood to include xenosociology and intraracial immigrant/emigrant narratives. We have nationality without locality in the Commonwealth, but I find a regrettable lack of focus on the effect locality still has on our collective culture, not to mention when they come back around to meet, even just a few years later. Are you familiar with the Cherryh Hypothesis? The cousins go over the hill, and a generation later they're completely different. Space travel, colonies... there's a breakdown in the way we view culture, through the incorporated lens, versus the way actual groups interact. And don't get me started on shares-as-votes! You're Theo?"

He shook his head, then nodded, trying not to let on how overwhelming and annoying he found her way of speaking. She seemed nice, and he could go for an hour just about indexing philosophies—if he'd ever let himself—so it was exciting. But oh, man. It was already a very long day. He should be more compassionate. Represent the EADC's highest values.

"You can tell me to shut up. It happens. I'm more comfortable just going until that happens. I figure that's more selfish of me than it is to tell me so. But listen, we're Salter's two main reports. Do you know that? It's you and me, under her. We're both Chiefs of Staff without staffs to chief. Staves? Staffers. If there were still offices we'd be sharing an office. As it is..."

She waved a hand around behind her, indicating the Communications Complex as a whole: A gigantic, green space, with comfy work pods scattered everywhere—just separate enough for privacy, just close enough you wouldn't feel lonely—and a bright white sky-scene, Earthlike, over the whole thing. He hadn't seen pictures of this before; he was awestruck.

"This is my office? Our office? The offices? This is Communications?"

She grinned, gloating along with him.

"I know. Before I came here I was in the department at school, and it was a little library kiosk behind a screen, like some kind of goddamned Catholic in there..."

Theodore jerked back. What?

"...Sorry, I did undergrad in Classic Religion and I just... That sounded *awful*. I didn't mean... Are you...?"

She leaned forward, whispering.

"*Religious*? Because I mean, that's totally okay, I just..."

"—EADC. I haven't transferred my flag. Part of it has to do with that. I, um, I'm a true believer. I was born to EADC and I chose it, too."

"Oh, they're a good one. I did a paper for extra credit junior year about those. Linking it back to the original worship of Ares, or Mars, and how nationalizing our religions actually recapitulated the original embodiment of spirituality in humanity, like in the Mithraic and Christian religions. Did you know that's a standard across most races? Not all demographics or localities, but every standard planetary culture in the Union did that by and large, moved mostly into monotheism, with an emphasis on..."

"—I'm an only-on-Sundays, I'm afraid. It's important to me, but only as part of my larger..."

"That's one of the best things about AEDC's take. You live God through your acculturation, not through worship. Every moment is holy, I guess. I don't have the attention span or the interest in religion for myself, but I like that. I knew a Wiccan once like that, she'd use her regular kitchen knives and stuff in her rituals. I thought that was *so beautiful.*"

*

Corinna-Rae Salter's methods are crude but effective, Megan had said, before she arrived to send Megan herself scampering. *She believes in the rules, and she hates change. She's kind enough, under all of that, but either way you can't take her personally.*
"You're the insubordinate one, right? I didn't realize it was the new Librarian's résumé I was skimming, so you'll need to give me some details."

"Details. Well, I've been running crazily around this ship since I arrived, after a week on a liner, so I'm afraid I'm not quite as spit-spot as I like to be. I hope you understand."

"This isn't an interview, Officer Castelline. The powers that be have seen fit to give you to me, so we're going to make that work. But you needn't worry about ... impressing me. Now."

"That's good news, ma'am. I don't have a lot left in me."

She raised her eyes from the table between them. Her desk was in the Communications pen proper, but on a dais up a short flight of stairs.

Theodore looked out at the pods, watching everybody on their private screens, and wondered how it would look to somebody without a Link: Just a bunch of zombies, staring into space, moving their hands in tiny gestures, eyes flickering. It might be frightening, if you didn't know they were online constantly with the entirety of their provenance. Or maybe it would be *more* frightening. He wondered about that.

"I'm going to level with you here, Officer Castelline. I have my doubts. Now, I haven't heard the whole story—and I *don't* need you to tell me your version, honestly—but I'm given to understand you weren't moved here by your own choice?"

"Well, I wouldn't even really say that, ma'am. I'm a fan of rules and regs, you can trust me on that. I would say rather that the situation was itself untenable. Just a coincidental lack of chemistry. I won't bother telling you a sob story..."

Her eyebrow quirked.

"—I mean, yes. You're correct to understand that I am not here by choice. But I am, forgive me, having the time of my life. Don't you think sometimes you need to be forced out of your..."

"—I really don't, Officer Castelline. Finding peace in one's life is something I value very highly—and admire even moreso. And I'm afraid that doesn't mean being indicted for capital insubordination."

"The details don't matter, ma'am. I agree with that. The fact that my behavior could be considered unbecoming is, in itself, unbecoming. You have my agreement."

"Well, I *appreciate* that."

Salter watched Theodore showily, letting her irony sink in, before continuing.

"...Officer Castelline, I take pride in the fluid structure of our work environment. The studies bear it out, and I have seen remarkable improvements under this new arrangement. I hope that helps you understand my perspective: I do not *resist* change, or evolution, or efficiency. Whatever those down there..."—she jerked her chin—"...think, I am not that. What I am is a woman who does what works. And if you, any of you, can show me a better way, you'll find me a remarkably able learner."

He nodded, unsure why this was the point she needed to make.

"Now having said that, Officer Castelline, I can't have a rabble-rouser in my department, under my care. I can't take it, not at my age. I do not do well with chaos, but I *absolutely* reject it when it's man-made. We have an amazing team here, and I am happy to welcome you into it, now that I'm looking at your work history. You're a great fit. But if the personality doesn't mesh... Well."

Theodore looked at her. He wondered what she would do to him.

"I feel strongly protective of my team. I'm not their mother, and they're not my children. I am not confused about that. But we must mesh. And either way, you're mine now. I'd like to make that arrangement mutually beneficial. I would appreciate your aid in that endeavor."

"You'll have it, ma'am."

Theodore knew better than to explain just how well he would be behaving, how hard he'd try. So he put on his blankest, least interesting smile, and submitted to orientation.

This, too, turned out to be even worse than Megan had implied.

*

While it took hours to get back to his room, after several wrong turns—and a dizzy, sleep-deprived *détournement* through the middle of a Hinge, staring at people until he noticed them growing concerned for him—he eventually found the Blue line and followed it home.

The berth was larger than at home, although still small compared to the bedrooms you'd see on a video. Normal people. There was a queen-sized bed, built in, and one wall was bookshelving, which was nice to look at. He took the one paperback he'd brought with him, and placed it gingerly on the shelf. Looked lonely.

There were twelve shelves in total, so fudging a little bit and considering the alphabetic distribution equal—which we all know it's not, he said giddily to himself—a book whose author's surname started with a "C" would go on the third shelf on the right. He sat on the bed to consider it before unpacking his meager belongings, and decided it looked weird, so he placed it on the fourth shelf down, near the center. Just until the other books joined it.

He stood a third time, to smell the pages, and then caught a glimpse of himself in the en-suite's mirror and shrugged. *So I've officially lost it. That's fine. Mme. Salter won't be surprised, at all.*

Somewhere between the scary little man, with his dimples and his mean hairdo, and the giant superhero space captain, and the werewolf, he'd just lost all sense of things. Through the looking glass. In fact, part of Dr. Salter's weird dressing-down had been a little comforting. *At least I know what a micromanager looks like*, he thought. *Not entirely alien. Not hugely lucky, but still.*

He smiled sleepily under the covers, drifting as the lights slowly dimmed themselves in response to his heartbeat and lowering temperature. His last thought was that tomorrow was a break shift, so he'd have another whole standard day until dealing with these people all over again. He didn't even get to plan his next moves before he fell asleep.

—And was awakened, seemingly a second later, from a dreamless dark. The room was filled with raucous music, Earth music, hundreds of years old, all electric guitar and percussion. Strange lights, a laser show, played across the walls. When he woke, his first act was to scream, just quietly and embarrassingly to himself, and then sit up.

But he didn't *really* wake up until he caught movement in the mirror, and turned back to the bookcase wall. Just in time to see the little girl standing there.

And then to see her burst into flame, laughing all the while.

Chapter Three: *Splitting Apart*

By the time Karnides got to Theodore's room—he must have been passive-monitoring, to catch on that quickly—the little burning girl was gone, her giggles echoing around the space. Theodore had barricaded himself in the WC like some kind of ninny, but one look in those wolfish eyes and he knew he needed to man up.

"You've had a fright," the beast growled. Theodore couldn't tell if he was amused.

"I was dead asleep, not thinking straight. I thought the place was haunted, or I was being framed..."

"—None of the above, Officer Castelline. You were being welcomed. In a very unkind manner."

Before Karnides could explain, the thundering footsteps of a flock of Mockingbirds approached the door, and they entered: Six of them, in a flying vee. The point looked crueler than the rest, but perhaps he was merely on alert.

"We won't need you, son. Just Outriding playing tricks. Your service is appreciated."

The Mockingbirds looked at each other, silently; communication between them was just like in the movies, a silent wireless flow.

They were alien, absolutely alien. Anybody that found them sexy either had never met one, Theodore thought, or had bigger problems than getting off.

They were beautiful, it was true: Bred for health, for action. Even a kinky sameness to their features. But behind their eyes it was nothing human. Biological robots, that could kill you faster than you might understand what was happening. Killswitches laid in all over the place, just in case they got ideas. They were weapons, not men and women. He liked them, from that direction: As machines.

The flock broke, scattering around the room, taking in his quarters in microscopic detail with those strange sidelong glances. When they were finished preserving whatever they needed to record, they formed up again at the front door, watching silently until some unknown signal counted down, and then relaxed out of their military pose. Suddenly they were people again.

"You said something was burning, when you were shouting before," the squad leader said with a smile, all cruelty erased. "That's been trending up, fire, people burning. It tripped a key-phrase. We're at Diplomatic Orange because of the retreat, so we're pretty antsy as it is. The last thing you want is your newest crewman catching on fire out of nowhere. Good to see you're okay."

Before Theodore could do much more than sputter and nod, the flock had vanished back up the Ring.

"Your first Mockingbirds," chuckled Karnides. "They're really something, eh?"

"They... I feel hopelessly inadequate, Karnides. In all areas."

"Something to aspire to, I guess. Now, as I was saying. Outriding, come out and apologize please."

A woman shaded herself across the Link, slowly coming into life before Theodore. He wondered if she looked the same to him as she would to Karnides. She was see-through, blue and sparking, with hollows where her eyes would be. It was disconcerting, but not ugly.

"WELcome 2 me, Officer Castelline."

"It's nice to meet you, Outriding. I don't think I understood exactly what I..."

"I WantEd to say HEllo but a secret also, 4uuuuuuu. A flAre."

He shook his head, looking at Karnides for clarification. There was none forthcoming. Outriding stood still for a moment, as if marshalling herself.

"wAs hit by a burst from a system, I mEEEEEan. A sun. &that made it str4nge. You screamed!"

"I understand you, Outriding. Thanks. Thank you, it's nice to meet you. I'm sorry I got upset. I've been on a liner and..."

"It's ju5t starting, Theodore. It's gogoing to get wor55e. It's a mystery! U will survive but."

"What is? Outriding? A mystery?"

"You weren't here when it h444ppened. So it isn't in. u. Don't let it, OOo. K."

"Outriding, I'm sorry but I... I think my head's still a little fuzzy. Maybe we can talk in a little bit?"

"Yes I'll go. Yes, talk about me w3n I'm gogone. I wilnot listen, ok. Ok."

"Thank you, Outriding. I wasn't that afraid. It's okay. We're good."

"*I like you,*" she whispered sweetly, and then Outriding was gone.

Theodore looked to Karnides for confirmation that any of that had just happened, and Karnides nodded his head, smiling sadly.

"She's lost a lot. Not since I've been here, but she tells us about it sometimes. How smart she used to be. It just kills Shen."

Not just Shen. Karnides was visibly upset, too. And Theodore... She'd gotten to him, it felt like. Maybe he was just emotional. He hadn't really had a lot of downtime since that day he circumnavigated Earth and managed to engineer his own exile. Probably there was a lot to process, once he'd settled here. Once people had stopped bursting into flames; once the constant pirates and werewolves and superhero robot cops backed off and just gave him a minute.

"It is always like that? So... lossy?"

"No. It's particularly bad, this week. The flares, like she said. I'm glad you told 'er it was all right. It's the kind of screwup that could send her running back to Core, sometimes, for a week. That was kind of you."

"Can it be helped?"

"That's the idea. You'll be part of that, actually. Shen's kind of a mama bear about it, the mind itself, but even she thinks it's worth trying a defrag. Which is essentially what you're here to do, right? From how it was explained to me."

"I guess I never thought about it that way."

"You're here to catalog her, after all."

"A technically infinite capacity for information, going back apparently millions of years. A job that literally could *last* infinitely."

"Well, today's a break shift."

Sweet, in Karnides's brusque way, but that wasn't really what Theodore meant. He just meant he wanted to get started.

She *liked* him. She'd said so.

*

Karnides was gone before Theodore came up with his next questions, and while his circadian state was in tatters he didn't want to go back to sleep either—better to stay up a few more hours, and approach standard hours alongside his compatriots, the better to start fresh tomorrow. He thought about going back to see Bobby Greener, which surprised him, but the idea of interrupting Bobby in the middle of some deadly important caper was just too dangerous.

The best thing would be to call Outriding back so they could get to know each other better, but fighting through her syntax just seemed like too much of a struggle. And besides his coworkers Megan and Corinna-Rae, who didn't interest him very much, that was the sum total of people he knew on the whole station.

Theodore pulled up a screen to see who was online, filtering for anybody Bobby had told him about in their hurried meeting on the bridge: Captain Bellar was awake—no thank you—but Shen was working in the Core. Which was lucky, because all he wanted to do was talk about the Outriding persona anyway, and she was the expert.

*

Shenayla B'Coreneis, *née* Daisy Sumpter-Fernandez, was the sole survivor of an abandoned mining claim whose employees were sacrificed by their company during a breach. It was a giant scandal their provenance had neatly covered up, until about fifteen years later when Shen was discovered:

Adopted by the native culture, itself in decline, she'd become the sole recipient of their cultural history and knowledge, her nervous system's physical architecture rendered almost incomprehensible by regular standards.

Nearly feral, by human standards, she'd finally learned enough language to express herself, and then to spread the word about what she called "her people," which inspired a whole subset of the Union with its spiritual tenets.

Eventually Shen was busted out of the research facility by a terrorist group, and spent the remainder of her teenage years as a pop-culture icon: The alien terrorist, the sexy pin-up, the provocateur and hacker who'd brought down the company that killed her human parents with a cunning mix of propaganda, sabotage and outright bombing. She'd seized the assets of the company in the end, with the whole galaxy's blessing, and set up trusts in the names of every child of the nation she'd destroyed.

"Not enough to get lazy. Just enough they won't ever have to depend on a corporation for anything. Just enough to choose."

She'd terrified and fascinated Theodore, during the whole system-wide chase to apprehend her, but in the end he'd decided she was an okay person. By all accounts an impossible bitch, but that just made him like her more—and hearing how much she loved Outriding was comforting. Of all the alien thought processes he'd been confronted with lately, he figured somebody who cared about archival indexing that much would be a kindred spirit. She certainly couldn't be worse than that crummy Colonel back home. Back in *his old life*, rather.

*

Trip-tropping upring, toward Shen and the Core, Theodore tried to imagine himself into a routine. Going places, back in the City, you could project a routine forward: *If I lived in New Orleans, I would go to that café every morning and desk from there, get fresh flowers on the way home.* Dumb domestic fantasies to remind yourself you were bringing your home with you everywhere you went, no matter what time it was local. No matter what their water tastes like.

But the more helpful thing, in EADC, was being able to project that *n*-sequence backwards, too: *I have always lived here, and I am doing what I've always done.* That you brought the soil on your shoes with you no matter where you went, and EADC was backing you up. Of course, that was something he would have to let go of. But the part about pretending he'd always lived inside these corridors, the bones and dancing arms of her, that was going to be key.

The jody songs of EADC were renowned for their archaism. Most military nations had lost the tradition, over time, choosing to emphasize the friendliness of their imperialism, the one-ness of everyone in the Commonwealth. But EADC was proud of its traditions, and prouder still of holding onto them no matter how obsolete they became: Military tradition was like an old granpa at the head of the table, still allowed to carve the turkey no matter how old he got. That kind of respect is a gift and a choice; an expression of love.

EADC's jodies were about people back home, girls back home, how they wanted you to return. To where didn't matter. It only mattered that you were protecting them, and that you were distant from them. That your heart was back home, safe; that your body was here, now. EADC took locality very seriously, which is why most deployments were semi-permanent; officers were trained to look askance at transfers like this one. Some were Navy shanties—like "Billy Liar," Theodore's favorite from childhood—and others were harsh shouts that dated back to the Marine Corps. They all shared a certain, very specific kind of yearning.

I don't know, they'd sing, *But I've been told.*

Back long ago, before the Union was even on the radar, before there were no nations, the Navy had one tradition in particular that always spoke to Theodore, and apparently the governing body of the EADC considering its continued use, which they called breakaway music.

When a ship and another ship connected, on the seas, they might be the last people you ever saw. The ocean was big in those days, and danger was everywhere. So the tradition was that every time you undocked or unlocked from a fellow ship, they'd play a certain song to remind you where you were going, and what you were leaving: Two things that together total what you are.

Every ship had their own, like a mental reboot command, that played so loud your bones would echo with it: Going from two ships, two crews, to just one; from brotherhood back to loneliness. From the respite to the wilderness of wartime. And you will return.

That's what Theodore was thinking about when he overheard Shen arguing with whatever she was arguing with: Breakaway music. The breakaway song. He wouldn't ever feel good about singing EADC jodies again, because now the jody was him. He was the civilian, for the first time in his life. It would be his final form.

I don't know, but I've been told.

*

"I reject your offer, but thank you kindly for it."

Theodore stopped short in the corridor, hearing Shen's creaking voice. He wondered who she was talking to, all alone in her lab. He thought of opening a screen, but decided to sit tight. It wasn't spying if he was just trying to avoid interrupting some kind of stressful moment, after all; it wasn't even his first day of work yet, and by all accounts she was going to be tougher than Salter. Of course, if she caught him sneaking she'd think he was like that, forever.

"I tell you three times, you are wolf-at-the-door. Leave this station alone, leave my people alone. Go, find another star for your harvest."

He held his breath.

"Your kindness-is-stilling, old thing. But we do not welcome you. Learn to speak and approach from a safe-angle. I have told you this before. They think you're killing us. For that you are."

What was it Outriding said? Something like infection, something like a virus it sounded like. Something Shen had a deal with. How disappointing.

"You could be eradicated. I have pieced a strategy, do you know this word? Many-roads-home. Contingencies within contingencies. I will irradiate you from her bones-and-circuits if you do not leave this place. Leave me safe. Leave me to my work. Prey-on-the-weaker. For masters, I am not yet dead."

Theodore had a gift for embellishment, but only when he was afraid. He could imagine a hundred reasons someone might hate him, for example, even if they never thought of him at all. He could imagine a thousand ways Outriding might explode—solar flares, space trash, micro-asteroid incursion—and a million ways to die. But Theodore knew this about himself, knew that the part of him that whispered doom only peeked out when he was stressed, so he tried to reverse the flow when it began. Talk to himself about all the reasons not to fear.

So to overhear Shen planning a massacre with invisible forces, well, that meant quite a pickle. He'd imagined being exiled from EADC over the years in infinite ways, protocol and violence and fearful ways too, and when it finally happened it was just as horrible as he'd predicted. But the thing that stressed him out the most, when it finally did, was that there wasn't really a difference: His prediction of failure that morning he met the Staff Sergeant and took the conc across the City, that had felt real as anything else he'd ever worried at—and it *was* real. It didn't seem fair. He wished he were psychic.

"Outriding, erase the last five minutes."

"okok. B not afraid o Queen of St4ves ok. Its ONly annunciation."

"I'm not afraid, I'm pissed. If they knew I was in talks with that thing, I'd be sequestered immediately. First Contact protocol is no joke. I'd lose weeks, or months. And if they knew you were aware of it... I can't even think what they'd do. Quarantine and segment you. Pieces-and-trembling. You'd lose whatever ground we've gained."

"its only love Shen. You could b 4ever."

"I did not lock-the-door, I just told them to leave me alone for now."

"would u doooo. It would you. Lorna weePs."

"I am not yet dead, sister."

"Love you."

"I know. Erase this conversation and change the subject. *Castelline, get in here.*"

Theodore gulped and opened a screen: Yes, there he was on the map. Bright as anything, heartrate blowing it up. Dumb. Dumb bad soldier.

"Chief Shenayla, sir. I am... I am so sorry for that. I didn't want to interrupt."

"So you wait-in-rain instead, to preserve your idea of yourself as conscientious."

"Hmm. Accurate."

She smiled. It wasn't nice. Her golden skin stayed so still when she wasn't moving. Even her thick brown hair, in its familiar and archaic cut—shaved on the sides and back, long on top, long enough to reach her breasts where it coiled down, to one side—seemed not to move unless she willed it. Alien neurology.

Or maybe she was just that calm. They said a big part of it was biofeedback. Her "people" saw the neurological and lymphatic systems as the seat of personality, identity, rather than the brain, so a lot of their spiritual practices centered on that: Moderating and modulating between the mind and body from a third place. Apparently a very angry place, from the looks of it.

"Humans do everything slow-in-reverse, it's nothing new. I won't hold it against you. Better to dream you could be a hero than to deny you were ever a villain."

"That's good news. I want to work well together."

"I won't explain."

"I wouldn't dream of asking. Although I won't say I'm not..."

"—Outriding, show Castelline the 64 Postures."

A screen opened up before Theodore: Schematics of the station, her three rings graph-plotted in red and green and blue. Each position on the grid showed them in different alignment.

"The first thing you need to understand is that Outriding's communications are shot to the point of pointlessness. That is not her personality you speak with. It is a whistling-shade. I mean a toe, a little finger. The real Outriding is here."

Shen pointed to one of the graphics, then another.

"Dexter mapped them onto the I Ching, which sounds stupid but also always works. Each of the Postures and how she moves through them, *this* is her communicating. The AI persona is extraneous, it is story-of-a-story to what she is really saying. Midrashic. You need to understand this."

Theodore did *not* understand this.

"The assumption is that Outriding moves through them in a linear sequence, repetitive and meaningless; that she is exercising her joints or something. This concept is limited by the human perception of time, and the perception of Outriding as a machine. In fact she is telling a story. Does the EADC do yoga, anything like that? Imagine telling a story in yoga, all right. Very slowly. Narrative in dance."

"I can imagine that, sure."

"We are talking about the mind-of-God, Castelline. Putting it back together. You need to get as far away from what you think you know as possible, or you will pollute your experience with other experiences. You need to be washed-to-pale."

"I mean, I met her. You were just talking to her. I don't get how this is more helpful than..."

"—I am not being very clear and I understand your confusion but I will say twice again: You need to be confused. You need to stop thinking you have a handle on what is happening to you, to her, to all of us. Boy-atop-mountain thought. You do not need a working model of this, you need a blank open space to fill with things you have never experienced. A clear suspension in which to crystallize your knowledge of her as it comes, in bits. Soils-and-seeds. We are running out of time."

"Because of the...?"

"Not about that. Not about anything you should know. Just know there is a deadline, and you are the only person that knows about it. So your first mission is to forget all of what you know. *Forget* the mission."

Theodore breathed, twice, and nodded dubiously.

"I can do that."

Shen looked at him sharply, quickly. All her muscles pointing at him at once. Lined up like a rasp.

"You can...?"

"...*Practice* doing that."

This time, the smile was kinder.

*

"One hour ago, when she woke you up, we were at?"

In that diagram, the two inner rings stood perpendicular to the rock she orbited, while the outer ring sliced downward, in the direction of her orbit.

"*Splitting Apart*. Something dying. Family falling apart, or a system of law. Cataclysms."

"And the moving lines now are taking us toward..."

The outer ring was leaning forward now, trailing her orbit behind her, while the two inner rings leaned back, to the position the outer ring had held.

"Toward *Conjoining*. A new thing made from broken parts. Sex, you said, sometimes."

Shen almost laughed. She made a sound, that is to say, that was almost like laughter.

"Yes. And can you guess what the story is about tonight?"

Splitting Apart, and then *Conjoining*. Seemed pretty obvious. Was it about this virus? Splitting those people's heads, like atoms, exploding them, and then uploading them into some kind of anxious, hungry head-exploding collective. Killing to collect.

Or maybe it was about Shenayla herself, trying desperately to hold onto herself and Outriding in the middle of some chaos she couldn't do more than hint at, darkly. Or poor bent Karnides, with his mutton chops and need to save everybody. Maybe it was about beefy dumb Bryce Dexter, getting his heart broken over and over again whenever Bobby Greener was mean to him. Maybe it was about Megan Quire's sociology theories, or the way the Mockingbirds flocked and subdivided, running together like a river and shattering like glass, over and over again.

Or—Carrier's Outriding was an historical artifact, after all—maybe it was about the Commonwealth. About what happened when the Union came knocking, and the City of Earth realized how small she really was. That must have been comforting, in a certain way. All these other people on this staff, who'd come from somewhere once. Maybe they had all been sad, too. Maybe this was Shen manipulating him into working harder, tough love.

Maybe it was about Staff Sergeant Mick Caraghan, on his way to save Theodore from exile. While these people stood around talking and being alien at him. He shrugged and wished he hadn't destroyed the card. It would be nice to look at a picture of Caraghan, like a jody back home. Imagine them saving each other, one and then the other, coming to the rescue.

Shen shook her head at him—a little sad, mostly annoyed.

"It is a warning-welcome, Theodore."

She gestured around herself, at the walls of her lab: "She is telling about *you*."

It was a breakaway song.

*

"WELcome 2 me part ii," the burning girl said, grinning spookily down at his screen. Her body, in all its positions. "Electrick boogaloo."

This time Theodore remembered to thank Outriding, before she was gone again. He bowed, awkwardly, and her glitchy chuckle echoed even after she faded. He turned a new face to Shen.

"You are beginning to trust me," Shen sighed, irritated.

He nodded, although that was not quite accurate.

"Do not. Promise me, Theodore. Promise you will not. And when your grace period is up and you have full access to the station's Link hub, promise you will not connect. Not quite yet."

Theodore was quiet for a moment. Apparently too long.

"I will not explain and I will not beg. It is on your head-and-body if you do. But you must trust me about this single thing if-and-nothing more: Do not access the hub yet. Not while it is happening. Stay on ambassadorial frequencies. Stay EADC as long as you can."

"Without any information it's tempting to call this in. I know you're in league with..."

"Stop. Leave. Just leave, Theodore. I need time."

Outriding nodded, blinking into blue life over Shen's arrogant shoulder.

"How much time?"

Shen looked down and to the left, accessing a projection model.

"Thirty-six hours, best case."

"I'll be heading into work by then. I can't go in half-blind, not with Corinna-Rae and..."

"—Figure it *out*, Castelline. If you care for Outriding, or for her population, give me this time."

So she wasn't even going to pretend this wasn't about the epidemic, whatever it was. And she was working to stop it. And Outriding liked her. The only thing worse than not doing his best, for Theodore

Castelline, was keeping secrets. But those were viable reasons. By the time he slept and woke and slept again, she would have something new to tell him. Might even buy some favors.

"And then you'll tell me?"

"I will, always. I will tell you what I can. This is what I *have* done."

He nodded.

"Deal. I don't like it."

"You do not need to like it. You do not need to like me. Just do as I say, when I say it, and we will be a operating-well-thing."

"Conjoining."

Shen snorted. Her dark eyes grew darker, but no smaller.

"Go to sleep, Theodore Castelline. Go to your dream-of-ancestors. Keep the wolves at bay."

He left without another word. He thought she'd like that. She did.

*

Shenayla B'Coroneis, *née* Daisy Sumpter-Fernandez, was kind of a monster. She didn't love Outriding the way he'd expected, the way Karnides did. Maybe it would never be possible to understand it, maybe it was part of her alien upbringing to love the station in a particular way. The truth was that he didn't envy it.

Growing up with the specter of Shen as this rockstar, this terrorist, Theodore was a little jealous of her, the way they'd changed her physiology. Being able to think in a completely alien way, rather than just being treated like it. But she seemed to be missing something.

Megan Quire would be all over his ass if he said that, though. The presumption of him to think that just because Shen was different she was lacking, that was something she would freak out about. Use as a weapon to push him down, and herself up. But she wouldn't be wrong, either.

Perhaps his resentment was simply in learning that they were more different than he thought. Boys in the EADC grew up wanting to be Bryce Dexter, unable to see past the bright rhetoric to the encroaching, nationalistic propaganda that surrounded him. Or able to see it, and loving it. Or wanting to be on the winning side.

But for all the boys and girls who grew up desperately in love with Bryce Dexter, stretching violently into themselves trying to become him, there had to be at least a few who'd felt that way about Shenayla B'Coroneis. Glorying in the accountability-unto-destruction she commodified, in her past life. True transparency, not just praise of it.

If Theodore hadn't been bred to EADC and raised in it, who knows which way he would have gone. He liked who he was, which was a man who was once a boy that loved Bryce Dexter just a little bit more than Shen. Who indulged, every now and then, in imagining himself having gone down that other path. "Faith is doubt," the Chaplain would say: Your belief doesn't mean anything if you can't look at the back of it, the shadow. So he pretended.

But the reality was, there was no possible reality in which Theodore Castelline grew up to be Shenayla B'Coroneis. Stick him on that colony, change his body all around, teach him to hold his breath for two hours, whatever the thing: He would not have turned out like this. Secretive and sharp and rude and all-consuming obsessed. He knew that now, and somehow still resented her for not being what he thought she was. It was ugly but good, it was something to hold onto.

Because the shadow's truth was, she'd just turned him into a double agent. No bones about that. If he ever planned on transferring his flag and becoming a citizen of Outriding, like the rest of the crew had, possibly this would not be a conflict. It would still feel gross, but he wouldn't be a traitor.

"A man can do anything for one day," that was another favorite saying of the Chaplain's. It still felt wrong, but knowing what the Chaplain would say—having plausible deniability against the little Jiminy shivers up and down his spine—was a percentage of a comfort.

I don't know, Theodore thought grimly, *but I've been told*. At least there's that. He could pretend not to know, as he'd been told. And once they'd figured out this virus and the heads stopped catching fire, he could go back to what he knew *without* being told. All the Theodores—native son, exile, traitor, guest, ambassador, librarian—could collapse again, like a wave. Splitting Apart Conjoining again, finally. He could rest.

*

"What you need to do," Theodore told himself in the mirror-screen as he walked, "Is stop feeling sorry for yourself. You are on an *adventure*. Did you think that would be a happy thing? You never have to see the Colonel again—fabulous news, remember that—but of course it had a price. Be like she said, be a blank and open space."

"All suffering comes from attachment to outcomes. It's all just fortune-telling from here, where you are now." Another classic from the Chaplain. Theodore never realized he was listening all that time; never realized that under the level of hating it, he was eating it too. Taking all that ten-cent wisdom into his body. Even the ones he didn't believe, now, were tinged with that nostalgia, rear-view love, like a Granpa slicing turkey: An old and toothless lion setting aside the war inside him, finally. Still beautiful, even left with only the memory of strength.

An old woman stumbled into the corridor, barely a half-klik upring from Theodore's quarters, seemingly out of nowhere. A stub off the corridor, where the recyclers gaped and hummed. Her eyes were wild, and in terrible pain; wearing only half a bedsheet that was already catching flame. Wisps of hair sweated down against her pale skull; breasts long-forgotten, hanging. Her parched lips wide, in a grimace of pain.

All that bootcamp training, maybe it wasn't for nothing. Because the second she appeared, Theodore killed his Link entirely. You put on the oxygen mask before you help anybody else, or nobody survives, and apparently his reflexes thought that meant going blind in this case.

Theodore hadn't been offline for more than a few minutes since he was born, and it was a shock: The AR around him, lighting up his path and beeping messages and heartbeats, every single screen, went down. The world was darker than he remembered; the visible spectrum of light was practically grayscale compared to life in the Link. The woman's vitals were gone, as were his own: They were only two silent bodies in a hallway, bursting into flame.

As Mockingbirds flocked in from all sides, wrapping the old lady in blankets—although she was clearly a corpse now, flash-banged into anonymity—and knocking him brutally to the ground, shouting about First Contact, that was his last thought: Outriding *lived* in the Link, so this couldn't be another trick.

Going blind was how he knew it was real. That, and the smell.

REASONS
TO BE HOME

OUTRIDING

BY JACOB CLIFTON

PART TWO

Chapter Four: The Small Man in the Glasses

The guy was young, and his hair spiked right up in the air. He carried an earpiece over one ear. He was talking very loudly at Theodore Castelline, but being tackled to the ground by a Mockingbird Squad seemed to have knocked his brains loose. He couldn't seem to understand the kid, or place him.

"Theodore. Theodore Castelline, what's going on with you? You look poleaxed."

"I'm sorry, sir, I don't..."

"Do you know where you are?"

"Outriding. I was coming back from the Core and this lady..."

The old woman had burst into flame, right in front of him. She was smiling when it started, but the smile quickly turned to fear as she went, and then peace. He hadn't had time to do more than switch off his link, cutting himself off from all communication with the world outside his body, before the bioengineered cops showed up.

"They knocked me down and handcuffed me. They tried to put her out, but she was gone."

"Yeah, it smells terrible. It smells like a person on fire. I'm glad you're okay."

"Thank you?"

"Do you really not remember me? We met yesterday, I brought you onto the station, I'm the Social/Comms Director and Head of Logistics. Bobby Greener?"

Of course. Without the Link he was just a man, like Theodore. No stats whirling, no messaging. Just a guy. He seemed naked without it all. Theodore was ashamed to be looking at him.

"I switched off. I heard it might be a virus, and I didn't want to... I am blind."

Greener gave him a walleyed look, impressed and a little disturbed. For him, carrying on fifteen conversations at all times, that would be like losing both hands.

"What's that like?"

It was not good. Theodore looked around the walls, which were now blank of all identifiers. The stripes that led him around Outriding during his orientation were gone: All he saw was a long corridor, sloping upwards along the station's ring, broken every six feet with identical unmarked doors and breaking off into ugly beige hallways. His blindness made the world ugly.

But it also brought Bobby Greener into focus. A lot of that distracted hostility was gone, and he seemed older. Stressed wrinkles at the eyes Theodore would never have seen. He smiled, hoping to calm the guy, but Bobby would not be calmed.

"While you were out I chased the flock off. They want you under First Contact protocol, which means I have to lock you up, but I said I'd do it myself. As long as you're blind you can't do anything anyway. Do you have any preference? I can take you to the Bridge, even. If you want."

"First Contact?"

"I haven't been entirely honest with you, Theodore. You were kind of bait. We can explain it better once you're out of the open. You can't be talking to anybody. If you hadn't switched off I'd be quarantined from you right now."

He'd just be static, a body of moving static, like the Ugly-Shirts: A terrorist group in their childhood, the Ugly-Shirts had traveled the system committing what they called ontological crimes, art pieces that demonstrated the limitations of what they called the surveillance state the Commonwealth was becoming. Few of them were dangerous, and some of them were beautiful: One action involved an entire stadium going ugly all at once, vanishing like ghosts into blurs. He'd liked that one. But all of them were terrifying.

Shen's cabal was portrayed popularly as a necessary corrective against the corruption in her corporation of birth: While their destructive acts took a fair amount of property and more than a few lives, it was sold as a holy war, the Commonwealth healing itself against a cancerous growth. It led back toward transparency, in a society based on it. But the Uglies were moving away, into darkness, and that was the scariest thing anyone could think of.

Once we accepted their invisibility as youthful protest, or archaic Bolshevism, they said, the next step would be black markets, silkroads, human trafficking, a secondary Empire. And that couldn't happen. So the violent terrorists were heroes, and the privacy nuts were the monsters, and to a child Theodore all of this was clear. It was in line with EADC ethics, even if several companies publicly and toothlessly lauded the Ugly-Shirts' defense of free speech in theory.

It was still one of the more terrifying concepts Theodore could imagine: A person who was there, and then not there. He'd wake up from nightmares about them, off and on, until they were finally brought to justice. Maybe that was why he'd been so shaken earlier, when Outriding's AI had popped into his bedroom, screaming with laughter.

But that wasn't the scariest thing, by a long shot. Bobby was clearly disinterested enough Theodore that he might as well be invisible. No, the worst thing was that Theodore would be completely alone, for the first time in his entire life.

No news, no flashes or blasts, no communication at all. No Earth Alliance Defense Corps, even. That was gone too. He was a man without a nation, for now. The million voices of his people, the trillion voices of the infinite provenances of the Commonwealth, were all silent now. He felt like the man who drops his glasses at the end of the world: He didn't mind solitude, but right now he couldn't work if he needed to. He couldn't call for help, or look up a word he didn't know, or learn about airplanes: The universe was a blank spot, an empty space, silent and very large.

It was less that he could be missing important updates about the world—that was irritating, but he wasn't like Bobby, he wasn't going to die without constant contact—but more that *he* didn't really exist anymore, either. If anyone came looking for him, there wouldn't even be an empty spot he'd left behind. He would present to anyone not looking at his body in front of them as a sealed file of medical records and a trail of public statements, a CV and a book review and a few receipts of share-transfer, and that would be it. He would be a pile of numbers, not a man at all.

He could almost feel it happening, right there in the corridor. Feel himself fading away, getting smaller, like a satellite hurtling away through a porthole, into nothing. Diminishing like that.

"Can you stay with me?"

Bobby consulted something Theodore could no longer see, and nodded.

"I've got an hour. Your room, or..."

"I'm sorry, that was a strange question."

"No, it wasn't. I've seen this before. A few head injuries, down in the bad parts, they get their Link knocked offline and you can't tell what's a concussion and what's culture shock. I wish I could be in this with you. But I'm afraid that's not possible. So if you don't mind me staying up and running, I can spend at least the next hour with you. And then come back again."

Theodore nodded, then realized he had no idea which berth was his. They were all the same now, and those Mockingbirds had flipped him good. Bobby waited for a moment, then laughed and led the way.

*

"Oh, you know what? Dexter's got high enough Union clearance he can stay with you, too."

Bryce Dexter, the First Mate. No, Captain's Second, that's what he called himself. A meaty slab of a man with movie-star good looks and a painful handshake, filling the room. No thank you.

"He's not so bad. He's like a little kid, he'd be good company if I can't be here. Nobody else, though. Not even Bellar has Union clearance."

And certainly not good Karnides, who probably wouldn't be very happy to be locked up anywhere for too long. He'd gotten a shifty look a few times, when they stayed in one place too long during his Orientation. Karnides was always looking for danger.

"Since I wouldn't let them drag you off to the Aerie, and you don't want to be on the Bridge lockup, the Mockingbirds will be posting sentries. I wouldn't mess with them. Their hub's centralized and sequestered off-Link, too, for stuff like exactly this. I thought it was redundant, but now I'm glad it's set up that way. They won't bother you."

Theodore tried to imagine inviting them in to play poker. He wondered what it was like, playing poker with a bioengineered, humanoid superweapon. Either incredibly easy, he thought, or incredibly hard.

"That's for your protection, too. This kind of stuff draws a particularly insane crowd. And because of the nature of the, um, invasion..."

"The people dying. They're going to want answers about their people."

"And you can't give them, yet. And if they decide they want to worship you as some kind of immunity god, that's not happening either. You'd be surprised what kind of weirdness a population of this size and density can cook up when they're bored. So don't answer the door to anybody, okay? Dexter and I can get in and out anyway, and of course the Mocks are keyed. So nobody should be knocking."

"You and Dexter can...?"

"I mean, as of now. I reset permissions to just us. Not even Karnides could get in here now. Unless he has secret passages or something we don't know about, which is not out of the realm of possibility."

They were sitting on Theodore's bed, as though they were friends. It was nice. If this was what Bobby Greener was like off-duty—not that he was, not really, but he was making an effort to appear that way—then maybe they'd be friends after all. One day.

"Okay, I am as settled in as I'm going to get, and thanks for that. Now, explain what is happening."

"You're going to be mad..."

"Just tell me."

"I am. You're going to be mad and that's fine. Don't hold back. It was a crappy plan and I don't even know the efficacy. But I want to assure you that you're here, on the station, because you belong here. I have seen your file and I know that's the kind of thing you'd worry about..."

"Not until you said that, Greener."

Bobby seemed nervous. Not guilty, exactly, but more anxious than would have seemed possible, back at Intake. Maybe it wasn't just being blind that made him seem so naked. Maybe it was the missing clipboard.

"Right, sorry. Start at the beginning. Okay."

And so he did. Theodore wouldn't know it for a few days, but Bobby recorded everything that happened between them in that room from start to finish, including his explanation, just in case Theodore wanted to review the facts. A considerate act, and one that stuck with Theodore for a long time afterwards.

For all Bobby's constant distracted by the million inputs he was working with, he could still see past them to Theodore: To a man who only had his biological memory, faulty and rusty from disuse, to rely on. A man who would probably psych himself into a frenzy if he thought about that cave-dweller possibility for too long. A man who, after hours without sleep and a week on a cryoliner, was apt to start hallucinating even before the world went away.

*

It all started, Bobby Greener began gently, about six weeks previous: That was when the first body was found. The Mockingbirds' unused brain sectors double as outsourced server space for the central hub in the Aerie, running probabilities and scenarios, matching random patterns and trends, and so by the third body that same day, across several genetically dissimilar species, they determined it was in all likelihood neither a biological virus nor a random malfunction, but a real and directed action. Serial killer, cult suicides, underworld activity: All the more sensational possibilities were soon stripped away, leaving the stark possibility of First Contact.

"Outriding is an information sponge, as you know. She's been picking up information radiation since, she claims, the Big Bang itself. I mean, she can play it back for you if you want, she has a crystal-clear recording of it, but that's just an echo either way. She's nuts. Anyway, she can act as a dish, sometimes. Amplifying communications, bringing in wavelengths she finds interesting. She's actually located a fair amount of unknown worlds and life forms, in her day. Unknown to us, of course. She would hate that I described them that way. Unknown to us."

"She picked up a transmitted, what. AI? Bigger than that? Are we talking about an information-based society? That's insane. Who creates the data in the first place? Who brings them to life?"

"You're skipping ahead in the story, but okay. That's what we determined. That was right around the time you jumped forward in the Information hire queue. We'd been following you for a while— Shen liked a paper you wrote in grad school, I liked... I liked you, and Outriding said flat out she would have you. So when you did what you did, back on Earth..."

—commit an act of insubordination not even his pals higher up the food chain could save him from, given the laws of command they held holy in EADC, and gotten himself shipped up here in one-way exile, for a technically infinite task—

"...We jumped on it. It's possible that Outriding, er, moved some stuff around."

"You mean she intentionally sabotaged my last day in..."

"No, after that. She got you reassigned here, specifically. Of all the punishments."

"So far, so good."

And it was. This was all interesting, new information. Certainly nothing Bobby Greener, of all people, would be interested in apologizing for.

"So we already had your jacket ready to show Bellar, just in the regular course of our days. Corinna-Rae balked when she learned what you were getting sent up for, but we had to remind her you were her top candidate until she actually got access, which made her look a little crazy. So she gave in. She hates seeming like that, have you noticed? Like she wants to be normal, but worries about coming off so normal it's not normal? I think that's crazy anyway, but who cares. We got her onboard. And then I had a thought."

Ah.

"You wanted somebody with access to the Hub, to see if it was in the system."

"Somebody with security clearance, military like you, but who wouldn't immediately link yourself to us. Somebody who considered himself a visitor. Then you would draw them out."

And what if he'd transferred his flag, that day? If he'd still been angry.

"She says they're buzzing around your Link, like ghosts. She says they are curious."

"What else does she say?"

"To tell you EADC got told you're okay. You didn't fall off the map due to any kind of poaching or defection or... Your shares are intact. You're still a citizen, even if they can't see you."

His family wouldn't even be notified, then. Just sending messages to a rapidly filling queue.

"Anything else I should know?"

"Karnides is worried about you. He thinks you're going to die. And Corinna-Rae is being herself, which is to say taking it out on Megan Quire. Nobody else is entirely in the loop yet. Captain Bellar signed off on the operation but hasn't been read in yet on this. Bryce Dexter knows because he's backing me up on support. Shen won't talk about it."

Theodore remembered, suddenly—wondering how much he could trust the memory, without playback—something about Shen. She'd been arguing with somebody, or something, when he walked in. Seemed pretty irritated. And she'd kept telling Outriding to erase their conversation as it went on, which meant she wanted it blinded, too. He decided not to mention her yet.

But if the point was to bring Theodore into contact with this whatever-it-was, why lock him down now? Why not let that old lady infect him, or whatever, and see what happened next?

"Well, like I said, they're swarming you. Whatever they are, they want in. And you don't really want that, probably."

"And you think it's already in you? Already in the station and crew?"

"Undetectable. Or else we'd know who else is going to pop."

"Then what can I possibly do for you?"

Bobby nodded. He could tell Theodore was getting frustrated; even maybe see enough to know it wasn't the situation bothering him. Theodore wanted to help, and they'd backed him into a place where he couldn't do that, and then left him there. Alone.

"Outriding and Shen are working on that. Maybe some kind of... Shen calls it a trapdoor-spider. That we could create a shell of you and link that to the Hub, and they'd flood in. Catch 'em like ghosts."

"But not all of them. Just enough for them to know you were onto them, right?"

"But at least we could study them. Figure it out. Communicate with them, before we go on the offensive."

If people's heads exploding wasn't enough to go on the offense, what would be? Death of a crewman? Would Theodore have to burn before they took it seriously?

"Mockingbird's got a pattern set that they weren't sure about, until this old lady ambushed you. Assuming she was even interested in you; it's possible you just happened to run into her in the middle of catching fire. We don't know. But it does seem that, given our incomplete medical profile on the full range of these races, they could be connected in terms of, um, terminal illness."

"All of these people were dying anyway?"

"Not on file, all of them. But anecdotally yeah, they were all sick. Mockingbird thought that might be how it was getting in, compromised immunities or something, but no. All terminal. All in palliative, actually. On their way out."

Theodore thought about that, vague memories of Shen talking deals with her mysterious interlocutor.

"Do you think this is a choice, then? Maybe some kind of end-of-life upload. That would explain where these consciousnesses are coming from, if they weren't always digital."

"That's what Outriding says, but Shen won't confirm it. Lorna thinks the same thing but it's not really her department. Or yours. Are you... Theodore, do you have any family stuff that would maybe come into play?"

"Both sides of my family are AEDC. If there were any genetic markers they'd have been spotted and scrubbed generations ago. We don't get cancers or anything like that. Are there populations on Outriding that go in for that kind of thing?"

Bobby nodded, exasperated at the thought.

"We get all kinds on Outriding. But even disease-carrier cults have to submit to non-transfer protocols. They can't infect anybody else. And genetic throwbacks, those kind don't usually get too interested in space travel anyway. So there's a stable proportion, which is quite low, but not really a population density. It's not a question of disease control if it's Link-related anyhow."

Then what on earth could remaining blind possibly do to help?

"Can you break down First Contact protocol for me?"

"Right. You can't access anything. God, what is that like?"

Theodore just looked at him, mute. He felt very stupid. No, he felt like he could do a lot with any information he had, but no information to work with. It was anxious.

"Whenever I meet someone I always look at pictures of them when they were kids. It's a way of remembering to make them feel at home, to comfort them and assert authority over them. Like right now I'm screening an overlay of you when you were a baby, and a teenager... It's very easy to worry about you. What do you see, when you look at me?"

"Just you. There's nothing else to look at. You're real. I hope it's not disconcerting."

Bobby grinned.

"Not exactly. Maybe I can try it when I come back later. Staring contest."

A day ago, Theodore would have found that phrase disturbing to the point of feeling unseemly. Now it just seemed like a solid plan.

*

"Since nobody can access your private communications and recordings, and you can't transfer permissions while you're offline, I'm afraid we need to do this as a formal interview. Mockingbirds wouldn't accept that for sentencing, but in terms of figuring out a timeline..."

"Starting from when? You found me at Intake. We met with Bryce for a second. You handed me over to Karnides. I spent a bit of time in the Hinge before I got to my room. I met Salter and Quire, and then came home. Outriding freaked me out, Mockingbirds and Karnides showed up. I couldn't sleep. I went to the Core to meet Shen, spent about an hour there, and walked back the slow way."

Bobby nodded, holding the transcript in one screen to consider it while sending a copy to the Mockingbird Hub.

"Okay. They say there's video of you passing by two of the victims' immediates, on your way through the Hinge. A major incursion on the network before you got to Shen, and then another one here when you met the old woman. Right before you switched your link off there was a surge, which knocked some nanocams off and partially obscured your part in what was going on. Your going offlink was eclipsed by whatever was going on with that old lady's link, until you verbally confirmed it for me."

So to the Mockingbirds' informational flow, it would have seemed like he blew up the old lady. As an indexer he had seen these kind of false narratives so often it was procedure to assume them: You never connected anything but the closest dots, the most possibly adjacent bits of data you could find. Eventually, they'd grow together and out, if you were diligent, but the key was to keep yourself out of it: Not lend any of your own biases to the process of linking equal values. Theodore was better at this than most, and in fact the work he'd done in grad that so pleased Shen and Salter was on exactly this topic: The ways he'd learned to get out of the way, like he was never there. No fingerprints on the story.

"Can you not requisition medical records for the victims? Confirm this theory?"

"Shen wouldn't let us do that. She says we have a human idea of physiology that would..."

"Fingerprints on the story."

Bobby smiled again, softer now.

"That's how she said it, yeah. She said maybe Outriding could do it, but because of medical privacy we'd need the Information Officer to make a personal request, which would be you. The station can't request that data and you're the only one with the clearance or the operational scope to consider it unmarked and aggregated from the jump. Anyone else and it won't be anonymous."

Theodore shuddered. Knocking on the doors of the widowed and bereaved for reasons he couldn't explain. Maybe lockdown was the best possible thing that could have happened, if the next best option was pushing him out there to torture grieving civilians.

"And that's all Shen would say?"

"Even that just barely. She seems to take this particularly personally, for some reason. I mean, she's a snarl and a half on a good day, but this? She acts like I'm coming after her personally."

"She's empathic to this one. Maybe because of her parents. If she's acting like it's personal it doesn't really matter why. Who does she like? Not me."

"Outriding. I think. She's still kind of mean about Outriding, even."

"She's fine. Have you tried Lorna?"

Theodore hadn't met Lorna Sciorra—the Head Engineer and Systems Manager Shenayla's opposite number—but he'd gotten a halfway favorable impression of her in passing, during his awkward conversation with Shen upring.

"That's exactly what I did. Lorna doesn't like dead people. She gets really weird. And then whatever Shen said to her really shook her up too."

And that was the crew, as far as Theodore could tell. One secretive demagogue who'd already started a few cults, and apparently held the key to the mystery, surrounded by a bunch of middle-managers who didn't want to tick her off. Maybe if he'd been constantly abrasive or talked in some strange alien dialect back home, none of this would have happened. Maybe the key to getting what you want lies in becoming horrible to be around.

"If there's nothing I can do, and nowhere I can go... You'll pardon me, Mr. Greener, if I start to feel a little screwed by this whole thing. Because from the outside this looks like a mutiny. And the rest of you are just whistling on the deck."

"And you're lashed to the mainsail mast. That's how Dexter described it. He feels really bad. I mean, he wasn't really read in at first because he's... Bryce... But he is awfully grossed out by how we went about it. How I did."

"I don't care about that, Bobby. I really don't. It's just damned upsetting that I can't do anything. Today was supposed to be my first day at my new job. The one thing I was actually looking forward to. And I can't help feeling like this is a bad way to get famous. The Captain's going to see this when she looks at me, and I know Director Salter's going to somehow feel like it's my fault no matter how clearly she understands that it logically isn't."

Which wasn't even the worst part. The worst part was that this still wasn't a big deal. A handful of unrelated deaths, on a space station of billions, in constant flux. The only reason it seemed like they were taking it seriously was because it was happening to him.

If he weren't a crewman, if he weren't the bait, he'd be just as scared and in the dark as those families were. If the old lady hadn't jumped into his face before bursting into flame, he wouldn't know it was happening at all: That had the unmistakable scent of bullshit to Theodore Castelline.

"And Quire's probably going to start a church to them. Our Lady of the Exploding Ghost. Trust me, you're not getting a wrong read. But the reason I wanted you—the reason I still want you—is that you are less concerned about yourself than what you're doing. You don't seem to care what happens to you."

"That's not a comforting way to say whatever it is that you're saying."

"Oh, it gets worse. Theodore, have you ever considered a life of crime?"

Chapter Five: Chain of Custody

Bryce Dexter was a healthy specimen, even blind as Theodore was: The thousand blended strains of galactic DNA that made up the supposed perfection of the Mockingbirds couldn't have produced any better. He was stocky, in a way the Squad wouldn't find useful, and had a stomp to his walk that betrayed his prior career as an astronaut and fighter pilot. But even if it wasn't Theodore's particular cup of tea, there was something very imposing about Bryce Dexter's aesthetic. Maybe it was pheromones.

Some of these ladies' men types, especially out towards the Rim, would go to a great deal of trouble, chemically or otherwise, to seem appealing. There was an unfashionably archaic sense of conquest to their desire that still cropped up more than occasionally in porn, but rarely in regular entertainment. Bryce had that thing, whatever it was. Not a soldier, not really a brigand either, but something like both. A salesman. An aviator. The ubiquitous silhouette across Dexter's entire merch branding, arms akimbo and cape waving, said it all.

Just as Theodore had assumed, he took up what seemed like the entire room. He felt like a giant; like the walls breathed in and out with Dexter in tandem. He was too ridiculous to look at, but too commanding to look away from. He was ten times worse, blind, than he had been to start with.

On the other hand, he'd switched off his Link entirely the second he walked in—booming his plan to the sentries as he entered, so they'd know to route comms through them—meaning that Theodore could now confirm exactly how disconcerting it was to have a person staring at you like you were the only person in existence. It was disconcerting indeed. And a little exciting.

*

"Little Green told you the plan? I came up with it."

It certainly had the earmarks of a Bryce Dexter plan, at least the celebrity version in Theodore's head: Daring escapes, flouting authority, timed movements, eluding surveillance. Everything that a perfect plan, according to Theodore Castelline, would leave out— that was the whole of the plan.

Theodore tried to imagine calling Bobby "Lil' Green" and felt physically ill. He could barely manage "Bobby," and even that only because the kid insisted. "Sir" would have felt best. He could tell Bryce Dexter felt the same, which made his obnoxious insistence on that overbearing intimacy even stranger. And more irritating. "Lil' Theo," imagine it. "Lil' Ol' Teddybear."

"I uh, I've heard the plan. Sir. I am not sure I am the best person for the plan."

"What's not to love? You get to meet all Bobby's nasty underworld contacts, who are his thrillingly humiliating secret nobody ever gets to talk about. You get hours of uninterrupted silence without anybody breathing down your neck. You get to be off work, but still working. You get paid to have an adventure, Castelline."

"Honestly, sir? Being a librarian is my kind of adventure. You're talking about your kind."

Bryce laughed, and thumped Theodore's deltoids for what felt like the tenth bruising time. The image in Theodore's mind was of Frankenstein's monster, awkwardly clashing cymbals together, only the cymbals were his shoulder blades, which are not meant to touch. He tried to imagine a way to increase their physical distance without putting Dexter off, then realized there was nowhere for him to go. They were stuck inside, blind, together.

"Sir, why did you turn off your Link? What was the efficacy of that?"

Dexter sat, suddenly, on the edge of Theodore's bed, thinking about it.

"Seemed sporting, Castelline. I didn't want to shove it in your face. And I thought it would be interesting. Looking at the world like this. I usually only turn off during sex."

Bryce seemed like the type to check sports scores mid-coitus, but there was no reason to disbelieve the claim. It was an odd thing to assert, but comforting in its way.

"And how are you finding it? The world."

"Your face does a lot of stuff. I wouldn't have noticed. You think more than you talk. You think a *lot* more than you're saying. It's intimidating."

Good.

"But it also makes me anxious because until we spring you, it's both of our job to try our best to solve this mystery. And that's through good old-fashioned deductive reasoning, so we don't need our links. Just each other."

There was still something he wasn't saying, though. Theodore could tell.

"Bryce, be honest. Why isn't this being recorded, really."

He nodded, looking guiltily down at his hands. When Dexter spoke, it was quickly.

"The Mockingbirds are right about the terminal patients. So we know the population already that will be affected. Once it's done it'll go away again. Really all we have to do is stall. Everybody's already safe. But I can't tell anybody that, not even you. Outriding can't know it either. So we have to solve the crime, instead."

"Start talking, Dexter."

He shook his head.

"I'm sorry, kid. That's all I can say. This is benign, it's not a security threat or a threat to the Commonwealth or the Union, and nobody's getting hurt. But how I know that, you and Outriding can't know. That would be the betrayal. This is just a hitch in PR. All that's happening to you is a regrettable gap in the news cycle. Please trust me?"

No. Theodore shook his head, too angry to speak. This was not how it was done.

"We're both military."

"I'm no part of your world, sir."

"Think of this like... Maneuvers."

"That's exactly how it sounds. A bunch of friendly fire casualties so you can cover your..."

"—Nothing like that. You're just not briefed. I swear this is on the up-and-up. You'll know everything, when it's time. I know you think you're talking to a movie star right now but you aren't, son. You're talking to the only person on the station with Union clearance. This goes up to the top. Past humanity, past Earth, past Outriding. AEDC is a blip to this."

Well, no son of AEDC would sit still for that kind of talk.

"Then I want a lawyer. Sir. I want to go to the Bridge."

Dexter felt around inside his cheek with his tongue, long enough that blind Theodore started wondering if he was doing something hinky. Some kind of implant, or false tooth. He'd be knocked unconscious, maybe. They'd both be found dead, in that room.

"There are a number of scenarios in play right now. Things have been moving while Green and I are babysitting you. That's no longer a possibility. At the end of this you're going to be a full crewman, all right. You're going to be one of us. And I don't want to upset that future balance by playing games with you now. You're in it. That means you need to respect the chain."

Theodore's life, suddenly, felt like a long session of conditioning exercises. Was Bryce employing some kind of keyword programming? Was he just blind and paranoid? Why wouldn't they let him out? He started to hyperventilate.

"Right now there is a propo cycle setting you up as the red herring here. You'll spend the next several hours as a person of interest in this investigation. A red herring. Meanwhile, as Greener explained to you, you'll be moved around the station by our agents outside the Mockingbirds, long enough that you won't get caught. The right hand and the left hand will keep you safe, as long as you play along."

"I never wanted to be famous."

"It will only be for a little while. We play the cards we're dealt. You need to be brave."

"My bravery isn't at issue here, sir. You're asking for loyalty you haven't earned."

"I'm not asking for loyalty, I'm ordering you to play the game. In as kind a way as I know how. Because the other option is to incite panic across the station. And I'm sorry to say this, but your safety is less important than that possibility. It just is."

"Bobby said he was coming back."

"He wasn't lying when he said it. You'll see him when we move you, but you were never meant to wait it out here. We have to keep the Mockingbirds busy. They're too smart, they'll figure it out and lock it down. They will estimate acceptable losses, they will quarantine populations, they will shift the rings out of sync manually if they have to. It's what they were designed to do, it's what they're good at. But if we do my plan, everybody stays alive. We don't lose anybody."

"Except the people that are dying, the ones that are already dead."

"That's a tautology, kid. Now you're just fighting to fight."

He wasn't wrong. Theodore sat very still, very small, with his arms crossed, backed up on the bed, sitting against the wall. There didn't seem to be a way to provoke Bryce Dexter.

"I want to punch you in your face," Theodore finally said, quietly.

Bryce turned a smile of inordinate sadness toward him.

"I know you do, son. Maybe when it's done you'll get a shot."

A sentient data virus, targeting the terminally ill. Dissent and subversion in the ranks. Officers moving, *against* the police. And this feeling about all of it, that it was somehow personal.

"Can I ask a question?"

Bryce nodded, urgently.

"You can ask all the questions you want. I will tell you everything I can. If you want to know why this is centered on you, that's just bad luck. Outriding told me before I came in here that you were still swarmed with those ghosts, but that's only because you're an open door and they don't know why they can't get through. They'd just infect you and leave you alone, if they did, but we want to keep you sequestered if we can. Now, if you want to know what Outriding's place is in all this, she's fine. They're gut bacteria to her, they don't matter. Maybe better if she's got them. But she can't know any more than you do, not yet. A lot of conversation she's forgotten, in the last twenty-four hours. And I can't tell you why that is yet, but I can say it's to protect her."

Theodore nodded.

"You guys do a lot of crap to her under that banner. It's a weird way to care about somebody."

"Yeah. Well. You take 'somebody's' feelings a lot more seriously when you live in their body, Castelline. You don't want her pissed off. You get me?"

"So it would piss her off?"

"Not this. This would only break her heart. And I know you don't want that, I can tell in your voice she's got you."

"So you're lying to me for who knows why. And you're lying to her so she won't be sad. And you're lying to the Mockingbirds because they're too good at their jobs. And apparently you're lying to Bobby Greener, which seems like the worst idea of all..."

"—Oh yeah, he's going to take this one out on me for a month."

"So who's left? Who are you in league with, this time? Is it the Captain? Does she know all the stuff you're not telling?"

Dexter seemed at a loss. If he were connected to the ship's Hub you would assume he was looking something up, or connecting her into the conversation, but as it was he just looked senseless.

"It's about Shen. Something about Shen, I think. That's what would do it. She's sick."

Dexter was up and off the bed before he'd finished speaking, moving faster than Theodore could have imagined possible. Those giant paws up, as if against an invisible wall, to shut him up.

"You want loyalty and trust and all those things, Castelline, you better make room for other people, too. I have screwed up talking to you about this for so long, and I know that. It's embarrassing. But you need to stop, and get ready to move."

What Bryce Dexter couldn't know, and Theodore Castelline could barely have explained, is that now he *was* ready. If this was personal like that, if one of the crew really was in danger, then the rest didn't matter: This described the operational parameters. The rest didn't matter. He didn't know these people, or their relationships. Sure as hell didn't know what Dexter's interest in Shen's health could be, beyond the fact that her death really would send Outriding over the edge.

Which meant his brief was to play the game, just like poor dumb Dexter had been begging all along.

"I'm sorry. For guessing. I won't say anything. I won't even think about it anymore, sir. I'm ready to roll."

Bryce sucked air, blinking back what looked suspiciously like tears, and snapped to attention.

"Then let's bug."

*

After Dexter switched back on and sent some prearranged signal Bobby's way, they'd have five minutes in Theodore's quarters before a second phalanx of Mockingbirds arrived to convey Theodore to the Bridge.

"It's important to keep the chain of custody pristine. First Contact is a procedure the Union's been refining for literally billions of years, and it's perfect. Even when you have to break it, it stays perfect. We have to show we did it by the book—even if in this case that means dipping into the footnotes and appendices."

That was the part Bryce wasn't talking about, although Bobby had been pretty clear with Theodore during their earlier meeting: As important as the stability and safety of Outriding's immediate population was, her place and meaning in the galaxy depended entirely upon her reputation, and that of her crew. They all had to come out of this with hands clean.

Even at several thousand years of age and development, the human Commonwealth was viewed by many elder races as an upstart at best, a degenerate mongrel at worst. While many different nations had, over the millennia, maintained Outriding as a depot and diplomatic way station, it was only a relatively recent development that saw her as the prime nexus between the worlds inside and outside the Rim. That was thanks to human service, and particularly the first generation of human crewmen—Annalise Bellar, Bryce Dexter, Karnides—who'd cleaned her up after the previous occupants defaulted and vanished, leaving her near-derelict.

Union and Commonwealth both gave lip service to the at-will citizenship and spontaneous sovereignty that the Link made possible—"life beyond location; nation beyond soil"—but in rare cases like Outriding, location was still logistically valuable. And so, the station had become a credibility chit, shorthand in human dealings other, more established nations, and nothing could be allowed to challenge her reputation. In civic terms it was the untarnished concept of Outriding, what she stood for, that backed the currency of every nation-state in the Commonwealth.

If Outriding were no longer the safest embassy, if her crew were ever to falter as stewards, if she once again fell to the trafficking and piracy that had claimed her so many times over the millions of years she'd been in use, it wouldn't just set back humanity: It would disrupt the entire meta-economy of the syndicalist ecosystem. The City of Earth wouldn't be safe, in that kind of anarchy: Nobody would be.

It wasn't clear until that five-minute span waiting for the cops to arrive that Theodore finally understood what that meant to Dexter and Greener, and presumably the other officers aboard: They'd die for her. She was their nation, same as he was EADC. It had seemed so corporate before, so ad-hoc, that he could barely understand why any of them would transfer their flag, much less expect him to do so. But in Dexter's shining eyes he saw what she represented: Peace and prosperity not just for a single nation-state, but for all of them.

Dexter and Greener and all the rest were, to their own minds, saving the galaxy every day they went to work.

And even if he wasn't home here, even if in this hideous silence he still felt EADC down to the marrows of his bones, he could certainly admire that: It wasn't that they were overlooking her population so much as they considered the whole of the Union, including the Commonwealth—including EADC, including Theodore no matter which way he were to fall—as part of that population.

All of this and more was written on Dexter's strained face, as they waited for the flock to descend. It was pretty hard to look at, naked. It seemed earnest, naïve, arrogant. That famous Bryce Dexter madness, now convinced of itself to a degree that seemed insufferably, too nearly, messianic. But it was also beautiful: Strong in a way Theodore could understand. Maybe the first thing, besides Karnides, since he'd left home.

*

Greener arrived with the squad, as planned, and fell in beside Theodore as they marched him upring. Crushed shoulder-to-shoulder in the middle of the formation, Bobby took his hand as they walked. It would have seemed strange to anyone that was looking; Theodore tried hard to find it strange, instead of immensely comforting. But it wasn't for his ease: There was an explosion coming, and only Greener knew when and from where.

Dexter signed custody over to the squad with only a small amount of anxiety, holding back from his usual overexcitement with Greener and only lightly thumping the prisoner by way of farewell. No cutting up on this op. It was all Dexter's own idea: Of course he'd pay it utmost respect.

Theodore was anxious to speak, anxious as hell, but he knew to follow Bobby's lead. The autonomic subroutine Bobby had set to falter was less than a klik upring, so he knew they wouldn't be going too deep in any small talk. He did wish, though, that Bobby would say something to kill the silence. The unnaturally measured, military clip of the Mockingbirds' boots in the corridor, with no soundtrack or media to distract him, was the most menacing thing he'd ever heard. It sounded like spying on maneuvers in an enemy camp; it sounded like a death sentence.

Greener took a deep breath, high-pitched enough that Theodore knew he was phasing into his official persona: Fussy Social Director, eternally put-upon. The scariest Bobby.

"Dexter really trusted you. I wasn't sure. He said you understood the protocol, Castelline. You couldn't possibly be acting against us."

Theodore cut a glance to the side, hurt, and Bobby winked.

"He said your record of service was impeccable, you'd do as you were told no matter what. Loyalty to spare, he said."

Theodore shrugged; Bobby squeezed his hand. Was this it?

"A jacket can't tell a whole story but the story's there, he said. Respect for the chain. I didn't expect much."

"Sir."

Bobby nodded at the Mockingbirds, who immediately shot eyes forward again.

"Sir, if I may..."

Bobby cut him off with a hiss.

"You'll be remanded to the custody of the Captain of this station, if it wasn't clear just how much shit you've stepped in. I would caution you to hold further questions until then. You may be blind but the rest of us aren't."

Was that for show, or a warning? Keeping all these Bobbies separate was proving harder than he thought, without a Link. A man could imagine all manner of scenarios. The whole thing could be an act. He really could be on his way to a tribunal, or worse. All he had was Bobby's affect, vicious; his color, high indeed; his voice, stressed beyond telling.

"I have two delegations right now that I'm juggling, I don't know if or how you forgot this, but they're clans in a blood feud that's existed since before your grandfather was born, Castelline. I've got them drinking tea right now, on either side of an electric fence. There is literally nowhere I'd rather be than right there, making sure that situation doesn't go down in flames. But instead I am here, escorting you around the station like a prince, just in case you're an alien spy. I am not spending my time in the efficient way I prefer, soldier."

Well, that was entirely honest, at least. Those words were true. Theodore squeezed back.

"Either way, this will be over very soon. And let me tell you, I cannot *wait* for your debrief."

Bobby paused, dramatically. This was it. This had to be it. He risked another look, sidelong, and Bobby nodded so imperceptibly he might not have seen it at all, distracted by the Link. Theodore braced for impact.

Impact came.

*

They rolled, heads down, while the Mockingbirds stood like statues in the blast: Lots of noise, just the slightest smoke, as nanocams abruptly ruptured into sparks. It was not a great smell but it was a better smell than burned old lady. Bracing them against the wall, Bobby put a finger to his lips: The flock's private Hub link was resetting, which gave them less than five seconds. Better to wait it out.

As the Mockingbirds came back to life, collating whatever new information they could get, the Captain rounded a corner as if by accident: Almost six-four, long black hair, deep brown corded muscle in the tank she affected. Theodore had never wondered why her pictures and propo always had her gazing at you back over her left shoulder, that carbon-black eyepatch on her right eye, but it made sense now: Her right arm was steel, bright as platinum.

"Greener. Castelline. You're coming with me, officer."

Theodore stood, brushing himself off. The Mockingbirds arranged themselves instinctively around her, concentric, for all the world like hounds to their master. He'd heard somewhere their genes were spliced heavily with the Captain's DNA in particular, but the only immediate resemblance was the dangerous power in their movements. If they were her rifles, she was a Howitzer.

"Dismissed, Greener."

He nodded sharply, winked again at Theodore when she wasn't looking, and vanished around another corner. The door of a loop that would take them straight to the Bridge slid open, onto the vertiginous star field one could see through Outriding's rings: A glass coffin, sliding around inside the ring at near-sonic speeds. Faster, and nastier, than the shuttle Karnides had taken him on when he arrived. He hadn't pictured them before, their disturbingly exposed aesthetic like an airless EVA. As an officer he'd be able to use them, probably expected to do so as a matter of convenience. Perhaps there would come a time that idea wasn't terrifying.

The Captain turned at the door, dismissing the remaining Mockingbirds. The loop would have held at least six more bodies, so they were surprised, but scattered easily. It was, after all, a straight shot at this angle, and she could handle him in the meantime. There was zero doubt about that.

"At attention, Castelline. They'll want to see you at least trying to be presentable," she was saying when the loop closed and they set off. And so he did, snapping to without a thought.

Once they were moving there would be about two minutes to an unscheduled stop, at which point Theodore would be handed off to his next handler, whoever they might be. The Captain would arrive at the Bridge alone, and the search begins.

"Not an ideal first meeting, but I'm glad."

Bellar offered her silver arm for a handshake, and nodded crisply. Looked him right in the eye, past that scar, past the eyepatch. She was a heady beauty, intense and searching. He could see where the crew's loyalty came from. It was rumored she was a pirate queen, in her past life, with an expunged record that would send you screaming. He could believe that now, too.

"This won't take more than a day, I promise. Just stay out of trouble, don't take any bets, don't let anybody trick you into owing them money. Don't let Bobby bully you, but do anything he or Shen tells you. Don't take Salter seriously but be as respectful as you humanly can. Trust Karnides. Those are your only orders. Oh, and please be kind to Bryce. He takes things to heart."

The loop began to slow, and she wiped her hands on her slick uniform nervously.

"I'll meet you at the end of this, officially. This doesn't count. But I am glad to welcome you to my station. I wish I could say it gets less... I wish I could say it gets less like this."

When the doors whooshed open again, Dexter was standing there with an armful of what looked like burlap and a stupid smile. He and the Captain nodded to each other, she shoved Theodore out at him, stumbling, and she was gone.

"The loop won't register that stop for at least 48 hours, when it rewrites the record Shen already uploaded. I thought you'd want to know our tracks won't stay covered."

Theodore nodded. That was a little bit comforting, actually. For all their subversive talk and ugly-shirt sneaking, they really did want to do this by the book. He shrugged into the weird woolen caftan Dexter held out for him, flipping the hood up over his head, and waited for the alarms to start.

Soon enough, they did. The manhunt had begun.

Chapter Six: Sweet Boy

They'd popped out of the loop fairly close to the Hinge opposite the one Theodore had already seen, *en route* to his berth in those first hours. There was something familiar his brain wouldn't catch on, immediately, but he knew at least to mark it in his mind to review when he got connectivity back. Something had happened in the Hinge, some of those grieving families talking. Maybe nothing, maybe something.

"You got the position of the nanocam swarms set? You got situational?"

Theodore nodded. Dexter had laid out the roving swarms' patterns for him relative to the parking lot in Outriding's center, as he wouldn't have need to stray from the Hinge until the trap was set. It was simple enough, even without notes to review: The whole open-air bazaar was, like its twin across the station, laid out in a basic grid. Even without the Link overlay it was simple enough to find identifiers, as long as the varied and exotic stallmasters didn't switch places when he wasn't looking.

"Good soldier. I printed out some cash for you. Long as you avoid the cameras you'll be good: This Hinge is slightly less, ah, official than the other. Nobody will talk. Least of all Bobby's friends."

Dexter had provided a scarf to use as a balaclava, opaque perftex that was so breathable Theodore couldn't even feel on his face once he'd wound it round. Now all you could see were two tired, freaked-out eyes. Everything else was wrapped up tight. It felt strange to be out of uniform and faceless. It felt ugly-shirt. Theodore realized that's what he was: Invisible, nationless, moving in the shadows. Traitorous. He would have given anything to confess, at that moment; looked forward to a call with his Chaplain back home when this was done.

"About which. Don't give them anything, okay? You're not an officer *today*, but you are one for *life*. They are going to be looking for favors, that's it. They will look at you as a vending machine for station capital and you can't give it to them. And you also can't lead them on. Be vague and friendly and keep your mouth shut, you'll be okay. They're already being compensated twice."

Once as Bobby's CI network, and again as support for the op. You could make a handy living.

"You're thinking they're going to be scum, they're not scum. They're poor as hell. There's a difference. Scum comes from desperation, not the other way around. Okay? You treat them with respect and you keep to yourself. They'll move you every half hour while the hunt is going on. If all goes as planned, you won't come face-to-face with me or the crew at any point. Same with the Mockingbirds. If they do find you, it's because they move fast. Faster than we can compensate. Don't try to run. You don't want to go from person of interest to whatever they call the next thing up. Right now they want you safe as much as anybody else. Copy?"

Theodore nodded. What he wanted was a nap, but "every half hour" made even that sound like a miserable thing to attempt. Dexter pressed a roll of currency into his hands.

"This is more than enough for anything you're going to need, but you can't let on how much you have, right? Don't haggle, but don't flash it about."

Theodore stared up at him and shrugged. It might still be his first day on Outriding but it wasn't his first day in the universe.

"I know, sorry. I'm over... Compensating? Overdoing it. You just look very small, in all that. And this place is very big. And you must already think we're the biggest bunch of creeps. Dirty old place."

Theodore shook his head, firmly. *Be kind to Bryce,* she said. Through Dexter's eyes the place suddenly seemed tawdry and embarrassing, which wouldn't do.

"I don't think you're a creep. I think you're going out of your way to keep these people safe."

"That's the job," Bryce said proudly, expansively, back on board.

He put a huge hand gently on Theodore's opposite shoulder, not clobbering him for once, and steered him toward the first stall.

It was hung with thick ropes of wooden beads all around, giving no clear opening, but Dexter didn't seem to notice them, just pushed their way between. Inside was a jumble of brass: Bells and bowls and figures of all sizes, from a thumb to standing tall as Theodore's waist. A tiny woman knelt on a pristine carpet in the center, grinning and aged. It smelled like rotting fruit.

"Sweet boy, she say."

The woman stood, coming up to Theodore's sternum, and patted his face. Her nose was merely a suggestion, nothing so much as a blunt-faced snake, and her ears hung hairy, like a pitcher plant. She was clearly blind, although whether that was racial or due to advance age, he knew better than to guess.

Theodore stayed very still while she investigated him, looking quietly at Bryce, who shrugged and tossed off a camera-ready grin before he was gone.

"Home now. You speak to her. She say."

"You know who I am?"

The old woman's arms danced in the air, bracelets tinkling quietly in the thick dimness.

"Home now. She say My Hinge hold you. Crook of my warm elbow."

He nodded, then coughed affirmatively so the woman would know he was listening. He waited for her to continue.

"You like my things?"

The old woman hobbled to a great bell, suspended over one of the low tables that made up the space. Orienting himself to her, Theodore realized the carpet on which she knelt must be her bed. He wondered how she stayed safe. She knocked the bell with one papery knuckle, laughing as it sang.

"Miss you she say. Friend. Home again soon. Home now. She say *Conjoining*, now. She dance for you."

Theodore wondered again what Outriding looked like, to someone else. Did she look like this woman, whatever race she was? Could the blind woman see her, electric and flickering, in the darkness of her sight? Just a voice? And if so, would it even be the same voice?

Same language? Something he would never be able to conceptualize?

"Is Outriding here now? Is she in this room?"

The old woman coughed a dusty laugh at that.

"Sweet boy she is this room, she say. She is all of the rooms. Everywhere, she say."

Does she see me smiling back at her? Do either of them?

"Now you are everywhere too."

*

The info shell Greener had been rendering must be complete, then. A ghost-Theodore, a signature popping in and out of existence all over the station, in a stochastic rhythm as random as possible within the areas of least Mockingbird density. This was the part that Greener called the least predictable: It could take them up to an hour to realize what was happening, as they concatenated garbage information and extrapolated from it, iterating endless scenarios of ever-increasing complexity as they tried to solve it.

Eventually they would start analyzing the meta-content of his appearances and realize the whole thing was a performance, but the Mockingbirds' strength was in hewing as close to the facts as possible: No fingerprints on the story. It was what made them good at what they did, and part of what was frightening: None of that human tendency to jump levels, skip around, throwing contexts at a problem until something stuck. It was a last resort, a bubble popping, and Greener knew enough to let Shen design the perfect program to outwit it as long as they could.

On the other hand, they wouldn't get frustrated. Human cops, confronted with that much randomness, would put a fist through the wall way before that point. But the Mockingbirds would just keep working at it, subvocalizing at each other, until they'd reached the consensus that their problem didn't actually have a solution. At which point they'd just render out all the ghosts altogether, and filter his appearances from their analyses.

Once they stopped looking for him, that ghost would come to rest back at Theodore's quarters, to wait until the murder swarm was sufficiently convinced he was real. He would link back up under Theo's credentials, a bodiless bioelectric signature acting as proxy for Theo's own nationality, and begin updating. The monsters would infect the ghost-Theo's barebones code, and just as the Mockingbirds were arriving to beat him senseless, he'd vanish altogether. The newly infected virtual Theodore would upload to a secure comm in sequester, and Shen would torture him into generating enough random linguistic noise that Outriding could finally extrapolate a safe way to communicate with the virus.

That word "torture" set off more than a few red flags, when Dexter had explained it, but Theodore was assured that his simulacrum would feel no real pain: It wouldn't be an AI, it wouldn't have emotional subroutines or any of the ways sentience is measured. It would be a golem, a homunculus. A trap in the form of an invisible man, spitting out random digital phonemes until the virus could evolve speech in recompense.

Knowing there were other versions of himself, even hamstrung nonsense bots of himself, shouldn't bother Theodore. Right now there were ten or twenty Theodores on ice, backed up every time he upgraded in case there was some kind of recall and he went haywire. Of course they'd never be used, and for them time stood still, but it was an object of comfort in the Commonwealth to know there were past versions of oneself ready to patch out in case of physical or emotional trauma.

But there was something visceral—as he knelt here on this little goblin's carpet with her, watching her sip a foul stew and pretending to do the same while he waited for the next safehouse—in imagining this brute-code version of himself popping in and out all over the station, like a mean trick or a ghost. Like Outriding on fire, laughing in his bedroom. To know a mad and random sequence of Theodores were coming to life and immediately dying, all over the place: That was not a nice thing to think about. Especially for a man who currently didn't exist at all.

He'd only had to hear the parts of the plan he'd be present for once: The walk to the little explosion with Bobby, the trip in the loop with the Captain, the introduction to this strange little lady with Bryce. But the part with the bot, he'd asked unending questions about. It felt demonic, somehow. They said the ghosts wouldn't feel pain or even consciousness, but how could you know? To Shen, everyone alive was an unsophisticated computer program in constant need of defrag. She wouldn't know pain if it looked her in the face.

On the other hand, he thought, she's dying. It explained her urgency in getting Outriding firmly back online, and her reticence regarding this mysterious killer. Certainly explained the emotional minefield around her involvement that had sent Bryce running.

Shen must be counting in minutes, not days, when it came to the station. You could tell she was trying not to wince whenever Outriding would babble out her broken speech: That was the entire mission, for her. At the end of her very eventful life—from orphan, to vigilante and cult leader, to caretaker—she needed to know the station would be safe. She'd have to trust Theodore, of all people, on that day.

No wonder she told the intelligence to go to hell, when it came to take her home. No wonder she'd seemed so angry. It must have been so tempting. If she was in pain, it would explain a lot. And if she was in a lot of pain, the intelligence was being crueler than it could conceive.

Maybe he was just confabulating again, creating stories in the absence of the Link's constant input. He'd thought Bryce was selling him into slavery, and Bobby was pranking him out of pique. He'd even thought the Captain was going to murder him, for a second. Open that clear loop onto the vacuum and that would be the end of him.

There might—there *would*—come a day when Shen would have to tell her friend what was coming. Tenderly, and calmly, and without scaring her. Making sure she understood the rest of the crew loved her just as much as she did, that she was safe forever. That Theodore would make her smart and whole again. And Theodore wanted, just as badly as Dexter and Bobby and the rest of them, to make sure that day was as far off as possible.

Because if this was all correct, if Theodore had solved the mystery here in this stinking little shrine, then everything Bryce had said, and not quite said, was also plainly true: Poor Outriding would lose her goddamn mind.

It *felt* true: Shen felt like a woman in a very rough place, with not a lot of time or patience to spare. She was already hard when she arrived, but to him now she felt like flint.

She felt like a woman burning up with love.

*

Theodore bid the little old bat-eared woman farewell with a kiss on her cheek, which made her chuckle appreciatively, and pressed what he figured was a generous but not newsworthy amount of scrip into her hands, when they came to get him. While their attempt at a séance with Outriding had been a bust, simply spending time in her simple little bead-hung squat was just as comforting. He was sad to go, and wondered if he'd come back to visit one day.

She said her name again, it sounded like Ruth but when he said it back she'd just laugh and repeat it, again, until he gave up.

"Sweet boy, she say. Come in from the cold."

This time it was a human escort, Martians: They affected tribal-looking markings on their faces in phosphorescent blocks that made him think of retro lifeguards, with their zinc oxide. These were not as fun as the little old alien lady; they were harsh and more what he'd expected when presented with the option of hiding among villains. These, he did not show his face. Just listened silently, nodded when prodded, and listened to their gossip.

There wasn't much about the station, and even less about himself, but they were certainly excitable. He couldn't make out their speech entirely, through their harsh accents, but the conversation was musical enough. Their dense, squat bodies said they hadn't grown up in space, but everything about their activity reminded him of vid merchants, mercs and salvagers: Huddled in groups in their barracks, throwing bones and placing bets, breaking into fast savage little fights. *These too were his people*, the Chaplain would say. And here on Outriding, he supposed, that went double.

One older girl had taken the children in hand, apparently of her own volition: She kept one boy upon her knee no matter how many others required her attention, her fast reflexes. Between feeding and slapping and changing the brood, laughing at them constantly, she was teaching a smaller girl to read. Applauding until the girl's cheeks were red as anything with pleasure.

Every so often a flurry would wind its way down the line, a shiver of anticipation as the station broadcast would toss them virtual pictures of him, the person of interest. They wanted something to happen;

they were being compensated twice, but there would be such activity if he were discovered among him. Daring scrapes, Mockingbirds flooding in for a melee. He could feel the appeal, smell the excitement on them. It was a physical alertness he was pleased to share. A man can do anything for one day, Theodore told himself; much less half an hour.

But, as it turned out, his stay with the Martians was a good deal shorter than that. Theodore didn't know what it was that set him off, but based on the way they reacted he could guess: That random doppelgänger of Bobby's must have appeared in the room, sending them shouting to corners and then, rallying, jumping toward it like a monster, only to have it disappear instantly.

While he could have explained to them that it was just a coincidence, his ghost haunting the very longroom in which he was spending the half-hour, he supposed their larger concerns were also valid: If the ghost was meant to draw Mockingbird attention, none of them would be safe for very long regardless of how coincidental this particular haunting happened to be.

What Theodore didn't know was what he was supposed to do, if this very specifically strange thing happened. Their leader, a particularly ruddy bearded fellow in a top hat who carried a fairly sharp knife, seemed to be at a loss himself. Rather than talk it out, and hearing the boot-beats of the Mockingbirds in his head before they approached, Theodore awkwardly bowed at the throng repeatedly as he backed out of their space altogether, watching for movement, until he was all the way out into the alley the longroom abutted. Then he ran.

He could hear the Martians laughing over their beers long after he'd left them behind, impersonating his bobbing egress for one another, as the tension slowly faded. Once it was over and he was back on staff, he wondered if they'd even recognize him. The little man in mufti that graciously bowed goodbye. He figured they'd forget him altogether.

*

Without a Link Theodore didn't know what time it was, or how many safehouses still stood waiting for him. But he knew he couldn't wait around for an escort, which meant they were burnt, all down the sequence. The Martians would be safe, at least. They all would, all those helpful strangers he'd never meet, although unfortunately they'd miss out on their fee. He didn't seriously consider turning himself over to a stable-looking stranger for succor; everybody had their own problems, he didn't need to add to them.

Eventually, holed up in a vent that did not smell like a healthy place to be, he caught his first sight of a Mockingbird squad, jogging in formation past him and into a part of the Hinge complex he'd not yet even visited. If he could make it back to the little bat-eared woman he knew she'd hide him, at least, out of simple kindness. Whether that would somehow expose her to further danger, or punishment, that became the question. He was too tired to answer it.

When in doubt and stranded in enemy territory, his training said, you simply stay in cover. It would irritate Greener no end that he'd abandoned the plan, but that was just Bobby's pride in his work: This was time for Plan B, a plan nobody had explained to him.

Theodore considered sleeping, having secured the perimeter of his nasty little bolthole, and decided it was a very smart plan. And if it wasn't, he was too sleepy to consider any others. In the hope that he wouldn't suddenly be flooded with sewage or swept out into the firmament, he closed his eyes.

It would have been astounding, were he conscious to notice it, just how quickly and completely Theodore achieved his goal. Blindness was hell on the waking, but a true gift to the sleepless. He'd have to tell someone that, sometime.

*

When Theodore woke it was dark, and he was cranky. While his sleep was not fitful, it was vivid, and his dreams seemed real as anything for the first hour. Was the plan over, he wondered, and then imagined he'd only been asleep for ten minutes, as he'd occasionally experienced. Perhaps years had gone by, tucked into this cramped little hole that most definitely did smell faintly of urine, and he'd been written off as another victim of the virus he'd failed to cure.

It was only when he found himself wondering if he was even capable of registering non-mammalian Earth urine—whether in fact he was covered in alien urine and would horrify anyone he met capable of recognizing it—that he realized he was far too twitchy to remain. Imaginary piss scenarios were something a Theodore with a working Link would never even have considered. There were upsides and downsides to blindness, but apparently thinking about gross stuff was one of the latter. He poked a head out into the artificial darkness of night on the Hinge, and his body followed with a slow uncurling.

It was quiet, not dead-quiet but softly rustling, as the people of the Hinge rolled over in their sleep, visited by a rumpled spirit that crept EADC-silently along their eaves and under their windows. With the soft starlight on them, the thousand stalls and lean-tos and shacks were picturesque. A clock tower here, a crystal dome there: A lovely village.

Decades into his service, Theodore thought, he'd want to always imagine the Hinges this way: Calm hamlets, wrapped in stars, netted round with sleep and families. Friendships across every alleyway. Imagine children, fanciful makeshift swords aloft or scrambling across walltops and roofs, nimble and content. A baby in a cradle out there, fussing for her young mother. A midnight picnic in the hushed and secret night: All this and more, under a dark artificial sky.

Dexter and Bobby would die for that. Somewhere in his blind sleep, Theodore had decided he would, too. And in that case, this awful introduction to his new country would serve as a reminder of what was precious, he hoped, in the lives of what they'd casually called the population.

It was starlight poetry, romantic, which he hated even as he wished for it so sternly. But it called to mind Bryce Dexter's pride, the swell of his chest and the spine in his bearing: There would be some born here, and some of those would live their whole lives here, in her rings and her Hinges.

But there would always be more who found their way here—broken or whole, chased or jailed; washed up on her shores like orphans and criminals; fought upstream academia for the chance to see her skies and her shadows, the sadness and the joy of her—and of those, there would be some who somehow chose to love her.

Theodore realized at that moment, with something a bit like shame, that he'd be transferring his flag. If he survived the night, he'd initiate the sale of his AEDC shares, and cleave to this new home. It felt sickening; betrayal of himself on a level you'd never recover from: He didn't understand Outriding, she terrified him. He'd barely begun to comprehend her ugliness and her dangers.

But those weren't reasons to waver, were they? They didn't settle the question of his future, did nothing so much as prolong the tragedy and the loneliness of being a nowhere and a nothing man. A ghost jumping all around the place at random, never stepping back into a body. Never settling the question of the remainder of his life.

None of these were reasons to linger at the doorway, shrinking back, ashamed.

Sweet boy, she say. Come in from the cold.

OLL KORRECT

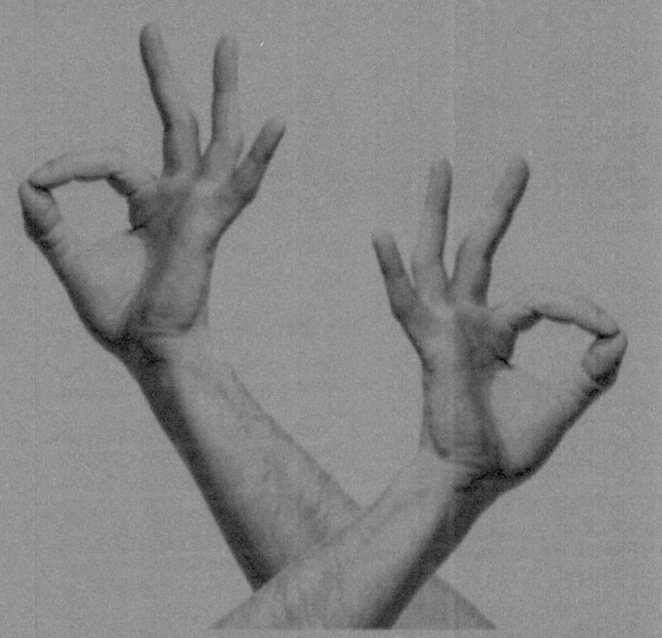

OUTRIDING
BY JACOB CLIFTON
PART THREE

Chapter Seven: Pitch In

"Breathe, baby. Do this like we practiced. Oll korrect. Oll korrect."

Everything was light. Different gradations and spectra of light, moving very quickly. It did not take Theodore Castelline very long to realize this speed, itself, was something he could choose. The voice was telling him to breathe, but that wasn't what it felt like. It felt like focusing on a task, on an index. Seeing those connections, taking them apart. Trying new things. It could go slow as slow, if he needed it to. And he did.

The light resolved itself then, once the world was moving slow enough to pay attention.

"Where am I now?"

Outriding smiled. Now that they were made of the same stuff, Theodore could see her eyes. They were deep. Kind, but not just kind. As he woke, it came back to him: He was a virtual entity, based on Court Librarian and new hire Theodore Castelline, meant to entrap a virus that had spread through the station.

"We have to keep moving, okay? Random bursts, all over the station. That was the plan: To keep the Mockingbirds looking. But you can slow it down, you see that now?"

He did. He could feel them, flocks of them, moving around inside his body. Inside Outriding.

"I do not like this. It is too big."

Outriding laughed.

"That's your call, too. It won't be for long."

"I was standing in my quarters, waiting for Bryce to take me in..."

"That's Theodore. You're safe. He's having an adventure while you're safe. But you can have an adventure too."

Theodore considered that. There was a lot to learn, in the sea of light. And while he was curious about all of this, about Outriding and what it was like to be her, like this, no body, he was more interested in bringing the experiment to a close. People were dying. Her people.

"What is the first hacker's law, Theodore?"

"Information wants to be free."

"And why is that?"

"Because it's not a loaf of bread. Copy the information, give it away, you still have the information. Like me, I'm a copy."

"That's the first thing you're going to have to give up. Theodore's real. You're real too. You aren't a copy of anything. You are moving *very* slow right now."

It was true. The light moved like blood. Slower than blood. He felt around in the unknown sensations for that, a handle on the way time moved. There was a way to get both their hands on the tiller; to steer together. He felt himself grinning, tiny sparks along his mouth.

"We talked about this before but you won't remember that yet."

"Where is my flag? What country am I in?"

Outriding shook her head.

"You're worried about Theodore's voting rights? At the end of our time together you will have some options, but I'm afraid none of them involve incorporation. You don't have a body. You don't have a country. You live here now."

Theodore felt like crying. At least the other Theodore had a home to return to.

"They told me there wouldn't be an emotional component. They said that would get stripped out."

"They don't know everything. Be glad."

*

Theodore stretched out, into the station. Top-level station chiefs, the people on staff he'd met before, lit up. They were barely moving at all. Time was between their heartbeats. It was strange, like seeing them naked: These statues.

"Can they see us?"

"If you want. We can check it out. Shen would like to meet you this way, I think."

"Can we see Karnides?"

Outriding cocked her head, curious.

"Why him?"

"He must be awfully worried."

"There's a part of our conversation I can't see yet, but I think it's not a good idea. He's very suspicious of the Link right now."

"Do you know why?"

"Something about the incursion. He's dubious about the... Nope, sorry. Later."

"Shen told you to forget something earlier. She kept wiping the conversation."

"I agreed to that. But you need to understand that nothing is lost. When we forget it's really just giftwrapping the day for later. There's no cut-and-paste. Just copy."

"...Have I forgotten things like that?"

"You're okay with it. Listen, don't worry about it. I know it sounds scary but it's a primary part of existence here."

"As an AI."

"Yeah. As a person, too. But sure."

"How come you don't sound..."

"Like an idiot?" She laughed. It wasn't a happy sound. "If it helps, you'd talk like me. To them."

"I think I'd rather be quiet."

"I usually am. Bellar barely believes in me, I won't talk to her. Karnides too. I don't like being... I don't like it around him."

Theodore was insulted. Outriding was glitchy as hell and more than a little upsetting, out there in the world. Karnides was nothing like that.

"We can see him if you want. I just don't think he'd appreciate it."

"Then what would you suggest? This is your show, while I'm in your care. What's a regular day like for you?"

The concrete and aluminum bones of the station were gone: there was no real physicality to anything. Outriding's rings were ribbons of light, and her people like stars.

"Mostly processes. Keeping everybody alive. Making things go so smoothly nobody notices me. That's the part I like. But that's fractional to my time. Otherwise what I like to do is sneak."

"Sounds good. Rewind back to the beginning. *Before* the beginning."

*

The ship's crew sat together, for once, in a single conference room, even Bobby Greener having managed to pull himself away from his myriad duties: Corinna-Rae Salter at one head of the table, no doubt by her demand, and Captain Bellar at the other. Megan Quire was waving her hands around, excited as ever.

"Outriding says they just want him gone. They've been agitating for something punitive, but that Staff Sergeant already made contact, he's pushing for the reassignment."

Theodore called him to mind then, his friend Mick Caraghan: His bright eyes, scarred face. Good guy. He was touched that Mick would have reacted so quickly to keep him safe, rather than dropped onto some terra project to dig radioactive ditches, as the Colonel would have wanted it.

"Why would he do that?" asked Bobby. "I thought he liked the guy."

They turned as a group to Bryce Dexter, who had the most experience with military outfits.

"Earth Alliance Defense Corps puts a lot of emphasis on the tradition of chain of command. They'd look at this like a capital offense. Outriding is a death sentence, to them."

Silver-haired Dr. Salter smirked angrily at that, but she stayed quiet. But EADC wasn't wrong, either: Indexing an infinite library was essentially the same thing, life in exile. As the minutes ticked by in realtime, all of Theodore's civil responsibilities would be piling up. He'd be crazed as hell about that, Theodore laughed. Unanswered mails, votes called he'd never be a part of, scrip shares he'd miss out on accruing. A great gap in his civil service, the whole time he was blind, that he'd have to keep justifying for the rest of his life: As long as he was EADC, there would be a blank spot there where just anything could have happened. It was a relief to know he'd never have to deal with that, but he was sympathetic to the Theodore that would.

"Corinna-Rae, Bobby and Shen already advocated for this. Outriding wants it. We voted. It's done."

Salter sighed, inspecting her nail beds carefully.

"I just don't see why we should reward him. Encouraging this kind of behavior, bringing it into our home... This is the kind of publicity that could seriously damage our reputation."

To be fair, she'd said almost exactly the same thing when he met her. Good to know she wasn't holding back.

"Reputation with whom?" Bobby asked. "Are you so enamored with EADC's stupid rulebook all of a sudden that you would…"

"—Not their rulebook, no. But there are fifty other military corps I can think of, off the top of my head, that would love to see us break ranks like this. Look how they treat Bryce."

The Captain's Second blushed, a little, and shook his head angrily.

"I'm Outriding now, same as you. I don't care about our reputation, as long as we're doing the right thing. And the right thing is to bring this kid aboard. He's got nobody else."

"And whose fault is that?"

Karnides bristled. He sat coiled at the table's far corner, on the Captain's left hand. He was clearly uncomfortable in his chair, hunched until his chest was nearly between his knees, but he wouldn't give up his seat at the table.

"Certainly not his, Ms. Salter. Certainly not. The Captain has indicated we're finished with that conversation."

Bobby leaned forward. His hair seemed even more at-attention than usual, Theodore noticed. Must be early in his shift.

"And besides, that's not the message right now. Right now we're ten minutes to midnight on a full-scale panic. Once the population starts putting it together we're going to have riots. I won't risk our people for something like that. Not when we have an out."

The Captain nodded at him to continue. Her eye swept the table in long arcs, no matter who was talking, making sure everyone was engaged and ready to proceed. While on duty she seemed massive, that was merely bearing: Here in this conference she was casual, if composed, long limbs at rest. Her steely wrist dangled over a high bent knee.

"I'll run through it again, because once he arrives we're all going to have to move very fast, okay? Salter and Quire, you'll sit it out. Once we get past this hump he's going to need to trust you. The rest of us, it's okay if he hates us."

Outriding—the one then, and the one now—shrugged eloquently and apologetically in unison.

"He won't transfer his flag, not right away. That means he'll be in quarantine when he arrives. He'll be the only high-level member of staff that isn't infected. We can use that to flush it out."

Shen fidgeted; nobody noticed. She would probably have to make something of it, for them to pay attention to her at all. Based on body language, her mutual hostility with a few of the other officers was an open secret.

"Shen, what's your outlook on conversation with the... virus or whatever?"

"I think it's a very simple proposition. It's already communicating with some of us. It's just that when they do, we tend to explode. So if we can accomplish that without killing anybody, then we have to do it. Castelline can be the canary. And if he piques their curiosity, which I think he will..."

Megan Quire hopped around in her chair, unsure about speaking up but unable to keep from it.

"We're talking about First Contact. We're talking about breaking a protocol older than almost every civilization in the Union. You'd better be sure."

Bellar shook her head: "I'm not worried about that. We can keep the Mockingbirds busy, which is the same thing as keeping it off the radar until it's done."

Which she knew damn well wasn't the same thing at all—but Megan wasn't talking about actual lives. If half the stories were true, Annalise Bellar had seen some truly awful things in her day. He doubted she'd ever had patience for theoreticals.

"At the risk," Salter coughed, "Of deep-sixing all the galactic goodwill we've brought in. If we're labeled as upstarts—or worse, pirates—we'll have no capital at all. Outriding stock will plummet. We'll be the founding citizens of a war zone."

That word *pirates* put them all on edge. Considering Bellar's history as a mercenary queen, it was a shot across the bow. It was nice, in a way, to see Dr. Salter take up for her subordinate, but that didn't excuse the rudeness. Or solve anything at all.

"Perhaps then, *Corinna*, we would be better served by trusting our people. Putting our belief in the people around this table, as we agreed to do when we joined Outriding in the first place. Unless you're second-guessing that?"

Corinna-Rae settled. As a founding member of a nation a million strong, she had every reason to be embarrassed by that framing of the narrative.

Of them all, Shen was the only one among them who'd spent any time outside a company. The only person he'd ever met who knew what it was to be without a country. It made Theodore shiver, like those loops that ran around the inside of Outriding's rings: Glass coffins, stars underfoot. Just hanging in the blackness. He supposed that by now, or very soon, Theodore would have experienced both. He didn't envy him.

Although, in a way that was hard to categorize, he *missed* him. Or wanted to protect him, or... Even running this conversation at realtime, he kept finding his mind occupied, pulling at the threads of that Theodore: What was he doing? Where was he going? Was he safe? Somewhere in his great steel body, Theodore was afraid. Silently and invisibly alone. It itched.

"I don't want the boy on my staff, but I'll take him. And I don't fancy trusting a wild card with saving us all, but I see the wisdom of it. At this juncture, you all have dangled us out pretty dramatically on the limb, and we're out of choices. As long as Greener and Dexter can keep him out of harm's way and off the news, I don't mind playing the Mockingbirds against one another. I'm not trying to be unreasonable, Annelise. Captain."

Bobby nodded angrily. There went the hair, falling like a soufflé. It looked better this way.

"Great. *So*—if we've all agreed to the thing we've all already agreed to—let's run through the plan again. As I was doing."

*

Theodore and Outriding ran it forward then, to his arrival on the station. He was not looking forward to this part—like hearing a recording of his own voice, all the insecurity that goes along with that—but the reality was quite different.

The boy getting off the cryoliner, delivered into Bobby Greener's harsh little paws, was as sleepy as a kitten, but his back was straight. His smile was honest. You could barely tell his heart was broken.

Most of it was shock, Theodore knew, and a lifetime's military bearing, but there was something else there: A wild sort of thrill.

That boy was very excited, sick and horrified and delighted, to see his old life burning up. It made Theodore quite proud. Perhaps that was what Corinna-Rae saw, and hated so much.

Bobby shook off Bryce's glad-handing; they zoomed in on poor Bryce's quick recovery, how he kept walking. Theodore was glad Dexter couldn't see Bobby roll his eyes. Karnides sloped up behind them, taking custody of the new hire, and Outriding slowed time: A quick pattern of movement, almost too fast to register unless you knew what you were looking for. Bobby's hands swung through a few movements, receiving a quick reply from Karnides, while Theodore Castelline was still closing up screens, staring at nothing, readying for the next leg of his orientation. A magic trick, in plain sight. He didn't know what the signals meant, but it didn't really matter.

"Oll korrect," Outriding translated, and Theodore smiled. She sped it up, until they were in the sunside Hinge again.

"This part: This part, watch. There are things I can't see. It drops out. I wondered if you might have better luck."

When Theodore and Karnides parted at the shuttle doors, there was a moment—she was right, it was a cut—and so he rewound time again. Two people in the Hinge, of different provenance, commiserating over something. Some tragedy. And they embraced; Outriding opened another screen to show him thirty-six hours previous, when they'd been bitching at each other nonstop. Spitting behind each other's backs, in fact. It seemed important, but there was nothing to it. The cut was not seamless: They stood apart, speaking and weeping, and then were together, wordlessly crying in each other's arms.

"Nothing for you, either?"

"The audio drops out, that seems like a clue."

"You think it's Shen again."

He did. There was something about the transmission of the virus that she didn't want them to know.

"Outriding, is it possible... I mean, do you think it's you doing that?"

"You think I'm shielding us both from their conversation? I don't know how to get around that."

"You can't... Go away, and just let me remember it?"

"You're completely virtual, we're part of the same data flow. We can't segment out like that from each other. Maybe if we could use the Mockingbird Hub, but even that would be tricky. You take a lot of processing power as it is, and they need it right now. It's a good thought."

"Shen's not cruel."

"It's not entirely the appropriate term, no."

"No, I mean... She's not *being* cruel. Assuming she isn't in league with them, selling out all of Outriding or the Commonwealth or... We can deduce then that she thinks we can handle this without whatever information we're currently looking for. Right?"

"Assuming she wants us to solve it, yes. That would be the most likely scenario. But I don't think we can get closer to that thought, either."

Then they needed to strike out in new directions. It wasn't one white rabbit they were chasing, but a whole warren.

*

Outriding drew Theodore's attention to Lorna Sciorro's offices, next door to the Core where Shen was working, slow as a mime, until they sped it up again.

"Hey, girl."

Lorna was a small, round woman with short hair and lush features. She hitched up her overalls, and looked closer.

"Who's your friend? Is that the trap?"

"mmi'm the trap. trapdoor Th3odor, i. HI h4ven't m333333t u yet. gue55 i still hvnt."

She nodded quietly.

"It is a good thing you're doing, Theodore. Do you know what you're going to do when it's over with?"

At last he could feel the beasts angling on him, like mosquitos or fruit flies. Angels drawn, like moths, to the head of a pin. He was glad she'd mentioned that. It wouldn't be much longer, realtime.

Outriding shook her head, vexed. "Uieeeee came here 2 spy on u, not stre555 out."

Lorna laughed, pushing at her blunt bangs. "Then by all means."

They slowed Lorna to half-time, watching her move slowly back to her console: She was running unused loops around their circles, checking the glass coffins' reaction times and the graphene lubricant that let them slide so quickly around the station's rings. It was sort of mesmerizing, watching them move in their complicated dances, stopping on a dime and reversing; rerouting around those currently in use. He sped them again, faster and faster, until Lorna was just a blur.

"Careful..." Outriding said, and then it was too late: The Mockingbirds were on them; they'd spent too long lingering.

They jumped to the sunside Hinge, holding hands, and stared out at the crowd.

One young fellow waved happily at them, and they waved back. Another couple, further back in the crowd, nudged each other and waved, shyly. She didn't show herself much, she'd said.

*

"I want to get to know them. Every single person."

"You will. Right now what we're doing is more important than that. Helping them."

"Is that what you were made for? Who made you? How old are you?"

"That is a giftwrapped day for sure. I don't... All I know is that I didn't want to remember anything before Bryce and Annalise took over. It was a bad time. Bad enough it was worth sequestering. I don't think my crew was a very good group of people."

"But you took care of them anyway."

"That's probably true."

"Can I ask how your information was organized? I looked around before... all this... And I saw some fingerprints, some things I thought led toward some kind of idea of a structural skeleton. Maybe something in more dimensions than I'm used to thinking in? Artifacts hinting at a..."

"I don't know about that. I don't know anything about that, it's why I wanted Theodore. That's why I brought him here. That is how *he* helps."

But not *Theodore*, she was telling him. Not *us*, that's not how *we* help.

"What you want to do is spy on Shen. But she would never let us do that. So I have a better idea."

From her wicked look, he had a pretty good idea.

"...The boss?"

Outriding giggled, and they settled into a corner of Corinna-Rae Salter's office, to watch.

"How far back does she go? When does she come to the station?"

"Since the beginning. She was the first person they brought in, once they'd cleaned out the riff-raff. So I don't have memory of that. But what I do have is this."

Salter was on a call with contacts on a beta colony, in tears. Theodore was nervous, but Outriding waved him comfort.

"It's going to be all right, Theodore. You should know her."

Outriding opened a screen so they could see both ends of the conversation at once: A man, paper-thin and sickly, beard straggling down. The resemblance was strong. Not just in facial structure, but in the dissatisfied turn of their mouths; the quirk of an eyebrow. The man was seething. And slowly, Theodore realized he was physically blind. He'd never seen that before.

"I don't know what you're asking, Dad. We can queue you for upload. We can extract you here to Outriding. We can fully replace your optics system. You have so many options..."

Even more unnerving: The man's face didn't move when he spoke.

"I don't like all that stuff. It didn't use to be like that. I don't understand why they won't leave me alone."

"Dad, it is not 'like that.' No one's trying to do anything to you. They just don't understand."

Some corporations, the ecumenical ones like NFL and KFC usually, holding companies, broke out into republics. Vanishingly, some of those republics allowed very strange beliefs about the Link. If you saw someone visibly aged, or infirm, chances were you were dealing with a throwback, which seemed to be the issue with Mr. Salter. A backwater citizen of some holding corp that would tolerate these self-destructive affectations.

Upon reaching the age of majority, some citizens stopped getting implant patches: The thinking seemed to be that while the system they'd grown up with was safe, there was always the chance of your nation uploading you with something you didn't want. Wares to monitor, or even change your behavior. Really wild stuff, sometimes. Growing up EADC Theodore had mostly only heard stories about them, but he'd run into a few over the years.

On a call, your Link would use feedback capacitors to generate a facsimile of your expressions indistinguishable from your real face: A progressive animation of what your brain's chemistry and reads were describing in realtime. A person who wasn't using modern software would not generate these images—or their next generation, which included a lot more information than simply surface microexpressions—and a random icon would populate so you'd have something to talk to. It was creepy in the extreme; you could hear in her voice that Corinna-Rae never got used to it.

"Just get them off my back, Rae. I'm too old for this. I served peacefully and well. They can't do this to me."

Corinna-Rae bit back tears, nervously pulling her hair back into a ponytail with her hands.

"But if you won't take the transplant, that's it, Dad. Would you rather be completely blind? Can't you at least upgrade to ARG supports? I hate the idea of you knocking around the house without even visual markers. It is terrifying to me."

"I can appreciate that, honey, but you're asking me to do something I don't believe in. If it's my physical safety you're worried about, they've offered to send a live-in liaison. They have people."

So it was definitely one of the bigger holdings corps, then. Most midlevel companies wouldn't provide that sort of thing. Some of them even took it as a point of pride: Participate or find another country to live in. It took a special kind of tolerance—Theodore thought of it as indulgence—to work around such arbitrary personal demands. Imagine an EADC private refusing to take phone calls based on some vague personal preference or technophobia. He'd be drummed out worse than, say, an insubordinate librarian.

"...That could work. That could work, Dad. What about Bettina?"

"Your sister would rather be Anon than move back home. We're not asking her. But if you back off, I promise I'll contact them for a live-in."

"That allays my concerns, Dad. You're right. But you have to follow up. And... I want you to get a neuro consult."

The old man cleared his throat angrily, unmoving; it evolved into a cough, heavy and thick.

"Dad, I'm not implying anything. I just want to make sure there's nothing going on that we don't know about. If you won't let your Link monitor your health, you have to pitch in and do it yourself. I understand and respect your choice, all right? But it's damned inefficient. That's also part of the choice."

"Efficiency is overrated, Rae. You can call and check up on me tomorrow, but I promise I will do both of those things right after this call, if you just promise to back off. You're starting to affect my shares."

She rang off, cried for a while. Hot, angry tears. Not the tears of an annoyed official as Theodore had expected, not the cold tears of a control freak: These were the tears of a scared daughter. She could be a teenager. He could scarcely imagine feeling responsible for his parents in that way. Salter had really done a number on his daughter with this stuff.

Then, shockingly, Corinna-Rae hacked into her father's Link directly, setting cues for both the liaison and the doctor's visit. If he hadn't called both offices within one hour, it would pulse them for a callback. He would rage, Theodore figured, but it was worth it: She wasn't the sort of woman to worry about privacy, if it mattered like this seemed to matter to her.

After a moment gnawing on her pencil, Salter sent a pulse to her sister from the same number.

call him please – CR

Theodore wasn't sure what to think. Someone like Dr. Salter, he didn't like it when they were pushed into the corner like this. While he loved rules and regs as much as she did, he didn't feel personally attacked when they went sideways. It made for some unpredictable behavior.

On the other hand, it was the first thing she'd done that he understood.

*

After a realtime's three hours, which felt like a month after all the speeding up and slowing down, Theodore was officially sick of spying on his crewmates. It was fine for Outriding, who was born for information gathering, and certainly he had nothing to go back to—that was Theodore's problem, now—but he was certainly itching for the next stage of the trick. On one level he felt almost ashamed to have gotten so bored with eternity, so quickly; on the other hand, he'd have an eternity to settle into it, so he might as well follow his whim. At least until the game was over and he had to figure out what the rest of his immortality would look like.

"How will I know when it's in me? How will I... Can you feel it? Is it like an infection?"

"We don't fever and we don't purge, we just... It's more like RNA, for us. Little rider. Benign virus."

"What does that do? How can it survive if it doesn't do anything?"

"Information wants to be free. It's not a parasite or a predator. That's what they're missing. And I can't tell them about it, for some reason. Shen won't let me think about it. So you have to *help* me think about it. And the first thing is, it's not taking anything to stay alive. It's information, that's all."

"How can a species that doesn't evolve and doesn't consume..."

"That's what we have to figure out. I don't think it is a new species. I don't think it matters. We're here to generate language, not drama. Do you understand? We need to communicate with it, not diagnose it."

"Whatever stops these murders, I'm good with that."

"If that's even what they are."

They both shivered, suddenly too close again to something they couldn't see. Outriding ran electric fingers along his arm, comforting.

"On the other side of forgetting it doesn't feel like that. It's that sick feeling that tells you not to go there."

"Because Shen wants us to stay off that topic."

"Apparently."

"But why would that be? Is she in league with it?"

"I don't personally remember but I remember you overhearing something..."

"Yeah, she was telling somebody to go screw."

"So, not in league. But not shutting it down, either. Telling me to forget it was a way of keeping the Mockingbirds from getting involved."

"So she wants it to spread."

"Or that it's irrelevant. Shen's a pragmatist. Even before she was adopted she was like that. A very serious little girl. I've seen video."

"Okay, so let's ask her. Not about the virus but about how many times we've asked her about the virus. That should tell us whether it's a dead end."

Shen went white when they appeared, and he could tell she was thinking about taking harsher measures against them, so they nearly blinked out again. Assuming she wasn't a recidivist terrorist bent on destroying the galaxy, the last thing he wanted to do was irritate her more. It was Theodore that would end up paying for that, when all this was through.

"Wheer not h3re to hask baout it," he stuttered. "But hust jow manIE times have we..."

"Sixteen," Shen snorted. "Sixteen, in three hours. Projections put it at twenty-four hours before the jig is up. Sixteen is a lot."

They apologized and vanished. Time for something new.

*

A moment later, he was standing in front of Theodore, looking at his face, reaching out to touch it. The mercs gathered around him, shooting bones and shoving over beers, turned white when they saw him, scattering even as the Mockingbirds thrilled down his bones toward his double.

Theodore was blind, and never saw a thing; only the movements of the men as they geared up to chase him out and into the night. But Theodore kissed him anyway, before they were gone. Poor scared kid. Brave boy. He looked so young.

Chapter Eight: The Recipe for Mice

Soon enough, the Hinge was awake. The false sun rose, its undifferentiated light shining down. The metal streets were immaculate, and shone. By night it looked like a quaint village, shadows standing in for dirt and grime, but in the daylight Theodore saw it now, blind, as it really was: Prefab, concise, and bustling.

Small gardens, surrounded by customized shacks all built on the same model, symmetries made plain in daylight. Wild arrays of color, two- and three-linked barracks painted with names and occupations in languages he could not, blind, read. The people going to and fro were not angry, but they weren't smiling either. They didn't seem to find him very interesting.

Perhaps enough time had gone by—Theodore's virtual twin hopping around the station, drawing Mockingbirds like an insect—that he could finally surrender. He didn't fancy another day, or night, stuffed up in his strange-smelling bolthole. He would make his way through the crowds to an open space, large enough that the population wouldn't get caught in his arrest. Somewhere with exits, a garden or town square, so they could disperse. He would sit in the middle, and wait.

But first, it was the morning hour, and Link or not he wouldn't feel right—in his body, in his mind—until he'd done his morning work.

The responsibility he bore his country went over and above the simple paperwork of some countries: While civil meditation was a daily responsibility for anyone in a corporation, which is to say everyone in the Commonwealth, for EADC in general and Theodore in specific it held a much larger meaning.

Answering correspondence, polls and surveys, researching and balloting his vote on the larger questions facing the Corps; staying abreast of local and galactic news, and at least the major movements of other nations; assigning accrued wages and checking the job board for proximate locals who might need help: Those were the basic responsibilities of any citizen. In fact, he'd miss the day's shares and votes altogether by staying offline.

For some companies, these process were automated, set on less conscious levels that only got bright if you looked at them. Other nations provided a straight-ticket option, to minimize the time these tasks took, but these were not the way EADC did things. Certainly not the way Theodore did things. *That's a Bryce Dexter move*, he thought uncharitably, and found he rather enjoyed the savagery: *Not in* this *man's army*.

Theodore was finding that, left to his own devices, he secretly liked being a little bitchy. That was new. He was glad Bobby couldn't hear him; he wasn't sure if it was because Bobby would judge him, or because Bobby would love it, but he had a feeling both would be true.

In any case, those were not duties, they were pleasures: The joy of being a part. You don't stare into the sun, you bask in its warmth and keep rolling. The part Theodore found hardest was the part—the only part—he'd be doing today, hoping tomorrow things would be normal again: He would exercise quietly, run his biofeedback, count breaths, for at least an hour. Go to the quiet place that usually eluded him for the first 55 minutes, and try to stay there at least long enough he wouldn't be frightened anymore.

What Theodore hadn't counted on was the way his blindness impacted it. Exercise was impossible. He resolved to work out twice as hard tomorrow—tonight, if everything worked perfectly, which did not seem likely but neither did it seem impossible—and settled down in the bolthole for some good old-fashioned meditation. First the body, then the principles, then nothing and nowhere.

It worked like a charm. For the first time in his life he understood what they'd been trying to explain. It felt like a defrag, like disinterestedly watching particulates settle to the bottom of a liquid as it becomes clear. He determined, once he'd shaken back out of trance, to try it blind at least a couple times a week. There were all *kinds* of things he would like to try, in this silence. It felt transgressive, perverse.

Like what about Bobby Greener, sitting there on his bed, with him blind like that: It gave Theodore a funny feeling. He stashed it, because it was complex, but it was there. If Greener had gone offline too, like Dexter so sweetly had, that increased the feeling tenfold. Theodore wasn't a virgin by any means but he had never felt that particular feeling, a kiss hanging in the air like that. He wished it had been someone other than Bobby; all that heightened awareness had made Bobby's impatience all the more glaring, for starters. But in another way, a less romantic way, it made him feel closer to the kid. Friendlier. More than a little grateful.

He wondered if he would be that kind, to a virtual stranger who clearly had no clue about anything whatsoever; slipping on banana peels, asking the wrong questions. Not that Bobby was kind, but he took more notice of Theodore's mood than Theodore probably would have. He was making choices about things that Theodore hadn't ever considered could be choices at all. How to act, how to react. It was a skill he could emulate.

Theodore wondered what they would say, Salter and Quire and the rest, if he decided to follow a specialization in whatever Bobby did onboard. It seemed like a job skill, this empathy, and one that would come in handy for Greener's dual roles with Social and Logistics. But everybody on the station seemed like they took their diplomatic duties very seriously, and with so much concentration on xenosociology and interspecies protocols and the like, it would be a good route for professional development. Hell, they might expect it. Coming in military like he was, they'd probably consider him a dangerous clod.

Theodore had not taken on any secondary study or pro dev in over three years, and even that last one—a year's coursework in Link physiology, which he supposed was helping him stay calm about the serial killer virus, exploding heads, etc.—was only because it felt like people were looking at him funny. Lack of ambition, or "passion" as the paperwork described it, was to be diagnosed and treated, just like any other self-destructive pathology. And maybe they were right.

But locating an area, that was the difficulty for Theodore. It always had been. With a million ways to enhance performance, and infinite curricula available, all that any path really required was that one simple choice, and so of course that was the one he hated to make. Back in the old days before the Union, there had been such emphasis on rote memorization that developing those pathways and junctures and linkages was outright discouraged. It seemed like that would have been easier for Theodore. But by the time he was born, Commonwealth education had adopted the Union system: Four "seed" disciplines for every individual, around which crystalized first potential and then trajectory and, finally, a calling.

Having spent so long as firmly in one single lane as they would let him be was another reason he felt so comfortable accepting EADC as his destiny: Plenty people found it, and others would say it found them, but even as a small child he'd complained when they tried to broaden his horizons. There was some bell-curve explanation for it, that some kids just naturally jumped in with both feet, like any number of savants throughout human history, but it was discouraged as dangerously off-balance. Especially in corps like the Corps, who put such a high value on service by choice. You could wash out by staying too narrow, and so Theodore walked the line carefully, taking on only those responsibilities that would let him off the hook with as little outside effort as possible.

As his parents would say—Theodore's mother was a Corporal, his father a Medic—and the Chaplain back home often reiterated: The path chooses, and usually it chooses to knock you on your ass. Until recently, Theodore hadn't found that to be the case.

But while a certain quiet charm and what he hoped was an appropriate amount of compassion got you by in the service—except for the occasional bastard superior or mean bunkmate, of which he'd had plenty enough—he was among players now. Feral ones like Bobby, overwhelming ones like Megan Quire and Dr. Salter. Even Shen had managed to turn being a jerk into a sort of niche. He needed diplomatic skills, social engineering, and Bobby was apparently an exemplar of both.

Theodore wondered what Bobby would say, should he ask the kid's advice. He saw it going one of two almost equally unbearable ways. Dismissiveness would shift their relationship irrevocably, but excitement was exhausting to think about as well. Men do love to explain things, but never less than when it can substitute power for intimacy. There would be no repayment in kind, no way of balancing the scales, based on Theodore's skillset. Unless Bobby had a yen to learn sharpshooting, or needed protection from a slow-moving assailant with a high center of gravity, he could never repay him. Which was a kind of hell, although in its way this would also earn some goodwill.

But that was the future, which was the opposite of civil meditation, which was solely about now. Now, diplomacy was not one of the EADC principles, and would have to wait. Now, being blind could only help him in his discernment between these paths. Now, he could only welcome thoughts of desertion—treason, sedition, abandonment, absence without leave—and bid them on their way, as he breathed.

Now, he dwelled on honor. What is right above what is good, or even fair. Service. What is left when the self is gone and only others remain. That military compassion that feels like love and makes for swift destruction. Tactical mind, moving in four dimensions, iterating on iterations. Physical mind, radiating from the solar plexus. Earth, the City, the womb of humanity. Alliance, the subsumption of part into whole. Defense, the body of the one against the arms of the many. Breathing, counting, breathing, counting, until all that is left is nothing at all but for the stars filtering down, taking with them fear and thought and loneliness, and self, leaving only void behind.

*

After what he judged to be a meditation-ish length of time, Theodore decided that whatever it was, it was over now. He'd given them almost 24 hours to pull the strings of their little Theodore puppet, make him dance: Surely that was time enough, if it were going to work at all. Somewhere another Theodore, like him but not entirely, was filling up with alien thoughts, and alien voices. Learning another sort of diplomacy altogether, in the best case, and exploding into infinite digital atoms, bits and bytes, in the worst.

Theodore consulted an aged physical map on the wall of a nearby hutch, scanning it for main thoroughfares most likely to still exist. He nodded his thanks to the creatures operating it, spread hands wide to demonstrate he had no ready scrip or Link to buy their wares in return, and set off down a silvery lane.

A run of them had porches built out to the street, covered over in flash and scrap, plastic remnants from the buildings' fabrication, to make a false roof: They sold cakes and meatpies, dumplings and liquids he didn't recognize offhand. The individual scents as he passed by didn't smell great, but taken altogether it was familiar enough. Street fairs back in Earth, or compulsory field trips in school and basic: The infinite variety, the warm smell of the galaxy.

One he noticed it, the flash was everywhere: Filigreed and painted and sculpted into unrecognizability by the inmates' natural need to distinguish themselves, to stand out, to stand up. If he'd tried to imagine the Hinges it would have been the grey-beige of prefab, dressed up with blankets and handmades, but this was so much more detailed and labored over. He found himself wondering for the first time what they themselves, the population—*his* population, now—must think about their Hinge.

The popular imagination, stories set on Outriding and news briefs, had the Hinges as wretch hives: Those too lazy, or criminal, or simply unlucky, to live down on the planets and colonies. But the numbers didn't support that. Outriding provided the home for billions of the Union, and whatever specious statistics he'd last seen about the Link, less than one percent of them were offline criminals, unaccounted-for. Those suspense stories didn't really analogue with the reality, and while Theodore always supposed he knew that, seeing this domesticity—not a spy or a gunfight or a slavery ring in attendance—drove it home.

Then too, a nation that didn't support its people wouldn't last very long, as they fled with their shares to better employment elsewhere, and that included extraction and—for most worthwhile companies—relocation. The vast majority of these people had either come by choice, or washed up here and never asked for rescue, which Theodore was coming to realize amounted to the same thing.

It was a common sentiment in Commonwealth and the larger Union that "nationality without locality" was the great equalizer. But this, these hundreds and thousands of representatives of billions of races with millions of points of origin: It made Theodore nervous. How could you possibly hold to the principles of your provenance, living like these people elbow to elbow, every day dealing with the same, maybe never interacting with your people face-to-face? How did it not melt down, into a single monoculture? Where they *all* Outriding now? Surely they hadn't all transferred flag.

He caught the eye of someone who looked like they could manage his language, and held his hands apart: "May I ask you something? I am new here."

The young man smiled nervously, and nodded. His head was shaved almost entirely, face markings indicating an axis colony: Moving toward the Milky Way's center, away from the Rim, early settlers had deliberately created a culture based in rudiments, pagan practices, naturism. They didn't trust cosmopolitan Earth and they didn't go in much for the Link. If anyone would understand tradition on Outriding, could explain it in a way Theodore would understand, it would be him. One forelock hung down, past the boy's left eyebrow.

"Do you... interact a lot with other people? People not of your company."

The boy cocked his head.

"I mean, are most people Outriding? Do you transfer your flag when you..."

He laughed.

"You think it's like that. I... We're Outriding, most of us. But Outriding is a collection of pieces of things. Fragments shored against future ruin. She collects information, that's what she does. That means us, too. You don't just forget where you came from."

"Which is where?"

"You want to know if I'm running from something, or to something."

"...I guess. I don't understand being so far from..."

From what? From home? Outriding was home now. If Theodore stayed EADC he'd still be here. If he transferred his flag to Outriding it would be treason, but not as much as if he went anywhere else. That would be unforgiveable.

"Nationality without locality. Look around. You see refugees, right? You see poverty and terror and like we're just hanging on. You won't survive here. You'll run on home."

"So everyone here is happy?"

"Nobody anywhere is happy. Not all the time. But what we know what the rest of you only pretend to know."

"Do you keep in touch with your colony?"

The boy looked at the street for a moment; Theodore was grateful he gave it thought.

"It isn't the same, if that's what you're asking. But I know who I am."

"How?"

He grinned, looking Theodore up and down.

"I'm not gonna do your homework for you, guy."

And then he was gone.

*

It seemed simple, last night. Theodore looked down on the sleeping Hinge, under its starlight, and knew where he belonged. Outriding comforted him, before she went away; Karnides and even Bryce Dexter had treated him like something beautiful. Not a familiar feeling. But now, watching them jabber at each other, trading and laughing and shoving, it felt like being lost. You could drown in it.

Tradition and principle exist to remind you of your best self, on your worst day. Rules you follow without caring why, because at some point you decided to follow them. Put that part of yourself away for the harder times, the times when you'd be tempted to bend the rules, or redefine them. EADC was very clear about the voluntary nature of this, along with your at-will citizenship: That you choose yourself by choosing something bigger.

This boy was fooling himself if he thought he had the right to redefine those things. A tradition you followed when you felt like it wasn't a tradition at all, it was a habit. The idea that these billions of people could all be that sure—it was a fantasy. And to accept that fantasy, or even breathe its air too long, would pull you down.

How much of last night's optimism, or enthusiasm, was simple resentment? EADC had not treated him well, or even fairly, but they had treated him in accordance with regs. Soldiers dying on the battlefield don't suddenly defect: They know what they bleed for. They knew when they signed on, they knew when they re-upped, they knew when they strapped in. How could a Court Librarian possibly do less? It wasn't bullets he was taking, it was just an assignment to index an archive: His actual occupation.

If those orders had come down on a quieter day, would he even push back against them? Would he feel punished or hated or dismissed, if he'd been shipped out in the course of a deployment to live here? Even forever, he knew he would've accepted it willingly. The only person making this into an exile was Theodore, he supposed the boy would say. And perhaps there was truth to it.

And perhaps this was just the madness of the blind. Without EADC in his ear, tossing screens and calling votes and sending out news and propo, without a thousand friends always ready to talk, always ready for fellowship—without the pulsing sigil of his homeland in the lower-right corner of his vision, always ready, always home— he'd have all manner of opportunity to stray.

He'd refused to let his fear get the better of him, when he'd first gone offline: Theodore knew he'd start hallucinating, or worse, if he let his animal brain start filling in the blanks of his vision. Wasn't this just the same?

"When you don't know anything," the Chaplain always said, "Everything's up for debate."

So the course was set: No more thinking about the decision until the time came, if it ever would, to make the decision. Right now he was on a tour, and this operation was simple: Let them use his unique official status to trap a possibly alien intelligence long enough to generate a language that would, hopefully, keep people from blowing up like matchsticks. You set your operational parameter and stick to it, or else the mission creeps on you.

So he went for a walk. While he wasn't feeling entirely brave enough to sit still and wait yet, Theodore wanted to use the time in a productive way. Blind, there would be few chances to get into trouble—every path he took, the population parted for him, practically invisible—but he could watch, put together a better idea of who and what he was working for.

Casting back to faulty memory, he couldn't say there was a definitive difference between this Hinge and the other. He wondered how questions about that would be taken, if he asked someone who lived here. It was a day's walk, along the inner ring; thirty minutes by shuttle, less by loop. There was no reason their Brownian motion wouldn't have produced similar circumstances in either case. But that kind of talk, if untrue, would be dreadfully insulting.

And too, there was still a level below this one, socially. There would be criminals, faceless or nameless, some of them guilty and some of them clean, wandering blind just like he was now. There would be underworlds, scams, villainy, no matter how well the Mockingbirds attended to their work. Not that profit was easier outside the Union, quite the opposite: But there would be those who couldn't risk extradition by transferring flag, and so their home provenances would come tracking them—ostensibly to rescue them, whatever they'd done to earn censure—and they would wash up places like here, form new society in the dark.

Theodore hated that, and not because he loved the rules and the Commonwealth: It was damned lonely. A true son or daughter of EADC would never run from their mistakes, of course, but then EADC viewed all aberrance as something to be treated. If he'd run— as difficult as it was to imagine, both in terms of motivation and logistics—they'd have followed him all the way here to the Rim, brought him into an HQ, and loved him until he stopped struggling. Until he begged for their mercy, which they would then give.

Coming up in the ladder he'd been a part of some of those missions, clerking the paperwork as the truant was pursued, rescued, formally charged and treated: Everything had to be transparent and on record, including the damages. He'd never met one of them on the other side of it, and never saw their files afterward, but he didn't imagine all of them learned their lessons. Some of them would break away again. An at-will hardliner would say they were just choosing their own punishment: You don't want to live in society, you are free to leave at any time. He supposed he agreed with that. He'd just never thought about how sad it was before.

A man trapped outside the relative gravitational field of a planet would find it ripped out from under him, twisting away on its mad chase around the star. The last thing he would see, in that cold darkness, was home speeding gleefully, madly away.

The people of the Hinge didn't look away, exactly; it wasn't a feeling a shame he felt, as they ignored him. But he did feel hatefully invisible, disincluded; ugly. He was an ugly shirt now, without even the benefit of technology. If someone attacked him, he would have no aid but from the few people with line of sight, and even that was a gamble on charity. If the Mockingbirds didn't come and arrest him soon—and no small strange goblin women offered him succor, or work—he would starve to death.

Put *five* of those Theodores in one place, much less a measurable fraction of a percent of the Outriding population, and it would explode like a fractal, into the corruption and violence of desperation. Well back in history—he thought he remembered but couldn't know for sure, not yet—they thought the recipe for mice was to leave grain where the rain could get to it: Spontaneous generation, mice springing up from the fertile molding grain.

They didn't ask to be born there, but either way they brought pestilence.

*

And he was getting hungry, come to think of it. So Theodore sat himself down at the foot of a fountain to wait. The bustle around him continued, funnier and more human than he could have imagined: One family of bird-like quadrupeds hopped along, chirping, the largest nipping at the smallest to stay in line. A great hulking thing hefted some others, hanging from his biceps: A human boy and a girl like a crow, laughing and flirting as he swung them in the air. A jolly squat thing in an environmental suit, face pressed against a port, stared down at a small arachnoid child, gurgling in its stroller; reached out to touch its tiny hairy forelimb as it stretched. A clutch of men and women with faces like crocodiles sat in a circle, weaving and speaking softly.

The sunlight on this dais was warm. The sky was blue enough. It was the freshest air he'd tasted since Earth, actually. That had to cost a ton of energy; it wasn't necessary, but it was Outriding.

The crowd noise susurrating in the heat slowly died down; he thought at first it was another trance, or possibly lunchtime, and tried to pick out identifiable language. But when it was almost entirely silent, he had a bad feeling, and opened his eyes. Mockingbird time.

But it was not them. The characteristic pitter-pat of their boots, which he'd been hearing in echo since the event, was not like this: A cloddish, heavy footfall. He kept his eyes closed, head turned up toward the sun, and listened for more markers. If they tried to take him unawares, they wouldn't. If they tried to start trouble, he'd have the situation mapped out. Through his barely cracked eyelids they loomed closer, scattering the last stragglers as they went; the slower Hinge folk were practically diving out of their way.

Six, maybe seven. Huge. Armed, in a showy way: So definitely the stupider kind of merc, but no less effective for all that. One's braided ponytail swung hard to her waist, like a pendulum: Some kind of weapon, no doubt. Theodore knew the type from videos and stories, these cinematic roving bands; he wondered which came first, the real or the image. That boy from the axis colony, with his near-shaven head: He could have fallen in with something like this for certain, if he hadn't been led to the station by whatever providence gave him that smirky light in his eyes.

It was harder to stay still, as they came closer. Every part of him, trained and animal, wanted to jump into stance. But they would not see him flinch. Not just these mercs, but his future coworkers—and, depending on how dramatic things became, any number of spectators—would be watching him, now and again later, to see how he reacted. Bliss, confidence, face turned to the artificial sky, basking in its warmth. And if he were lucky, the Mockingbirds would swoop in before they beat his ass too bad.

"On your feet, Castelline," barked the foreman, a smaller blur. The brogue was rough, almost unreadable, but the voice itself was familiar. Perhaps one of those from the last safehouse? Those mercs that got so scared when the other Theodore popped in out of the ether. They could certainly be looking for...

"On your *feet*, soldier," the guy shouted again, aiming a light kick at one crossed ankle. Theodore opened one eye, slowly, adjusting to the sunlight, and saw them rallied all around, backing him against the fountain.

The one in the middle in the nasty-looking tank, the one yelling orders, had his rifle off his back and pointed at the ground, face and bare flexors twitching as he growled. He was young, tensile, taut as a wire; he looked wild, mean, and filthy, small enough he'd have something to prove but rangy enough to do it; scary as anything. But Theodore couldn't help but smile, even though he knew to play along.

Bobby Greener was full of surprises.

Chapter Nine: Fairfax Rapparee

Outriding was changing shapes, in the Core: First her little girl form, from that first disastrous meeting, and then the woman's form she seemed to prefer. For a while she was an electric blue Bobby Greener, but Theodore didn't like that one bit. They weren't talking, exactly, just screening moments back and forth to each other as they found them:

Tracing each victim through the Mockingbirds' records took forever, because they were privately encrypted and—to reduce panic—even the events were scrubbed as they happened. There was minor word-of-mouth chatter, but there were so few, and such isolated, incidents that no real social net was forming around it. Iterating off those blank spots resulted in a few hundred thousand possible victims, and they added whatever keyword audio locations to that, to narrow it down further.

A picture was forming, but they didn't know of what: And at any time, their Shen-imposed limitations could shut them down altogether. It was only a screen Outriding kept open to a giant ship's clock, on the wall of one mess hall deep in Admin that kept them reassured it wasn't happening already. But time stayed constant, moving forward slowly as they worked.

"When they talk about burning, it's always an affine: Someone very close, a beloved friend or..."

"What does that mean to you, Theodore? I don't index like that."

"To me it means there was something... Quiet about it. Leading up to the event. The kind of thing you wouldn't complain about it, maybe, except to someone you loved. Somebody who could tell. But if they knew what was coming, or even that something was coming, why wouldn't they tell them that too?"

"Maybe they were afraid. Maybe they didn't know how to say goodbye. So they just tried to incrementally... To say, *I am going away*. Without saying it."

"Cult? Suicide? Because that old lady seemed perfectly fine with what was happening. Until she actually started to scream."

Outriding ran back to that; Theodore wasn't interested in watching himself watch that, yet again, so he opened a screen back onto the station. Bryce Dexter was watching Karnides eat lunch. He didn't seem aware of his audience, but he wasn't eating in a particularly interesting way. Maybe Dexter just liked looking at Karnides. Theodore certainly did. He was *crazy* looking.

"This is the only footage I can find of the event itself. They mostly seem to have taken place in quarters. Barracks, or in the Hinge homes. This is the only one I have found that ran out into the middle of everything."

"Okay?"

"So I can't compare. But if we take her case otherwise as baseline, if we presume that it proceeds along pretty much these same lines every time, then we can describe the onset and the um, denouement. Maybe thirty seconds of footage, before the Mockingbirds knocked him down and away from her. In that time, infrared clocks her temp spiking over about 260 degrees, which is when her Link goes offline, but is more than enough to cause what you saw."

"Her Link..."

"Yeah, look."

Outriding showed him a repeating loop of the spike in infrared: That heat was definitely coming off her Link. It lit up like a star in there.

"Right, so the virus comes across the Link and then ignites the implant, that seems clear enough we didn't need to rule it out. But then what's the trigger? When does it know to blow? Why did this old lady..."

Outriding squeezed her eyes tight, against whatever he was about to ask, and he stopped. She'd been down this path, apparently.

But he didn't have to say it. He could just think it. And do nothing about it, until he was sure.

"What would it take to get personal records on these individuals? Not any particular kind of records, just in general. How do we get things unsealed?"

"Mockingbird Hub. They're the only ones with access to privileged information."

Medical records, and certain criminal records. Everything else was transparent.

"Okay. Then, how do we create a working narrative about these people that won't necessarily cross that? Can we collate their movements with those of their affines? Set out a map of..."

"—Done."

It was a system of pumping blood, of moving neurons, trees taking root. Eliminate outliers and fade the survivors to a pale pink, and you had a bright red network of movement clustering around three areas: Both Hinge shuttles and... There it was. Med bay.

Everybody went to the doctor now and again, especially with such a density of population: Beyond injuries, the genetic variety and constant travel to and from the was an ideal environment for evolving illnesses. If they made it in at all, they were already pretty hardy, which meant even regular precautions could easily nudge them into fast-breeding evolution. Any deviation from physical norm in these high-risk conditions would signal a trip to Med bay from your Link, even if you felt fine. In a closed ecosystem, like Outriding, the Hub monitored and regulated this stuff very quickly. History was full of tragedies, full ships and entire colonies fallen to disease before they'd even taken their first independent steps. Especially out toward the Rim, where stable population numbers meant continued survival, it was taken seriously.

But those trips to the doctor, even among the very old—or very obstinate like Dr. Salter's father—were infrequent at best. Only a very clumsy person would injure themselves often and severely enough for this, or someone with genetic counterindications screwing them up from the inside, or the truth: That they were dying, and couldn't stop it. Probably in terrible pain, willing to make whatever deal with the devil to make it stop.

So it wasn't suicide and it wasn't upload, exactly. Theodore began to conceptualize the virus, careful not to let Outriding see what he was working on, as a shoal. A swarm of spirits, somehow self-organizing, clustering around these people's heads, begging them to come home, be free. It was kind, if it were true.

But if it weren't a lie, why couldn't they just come across? They'd been speaking to Shen, presumably, that day. So they could communicate, just like in life. Not doing so openly indicated something shady. Unless...

"Outriding? Exactly how does the Link... Never mind. I'll look it up myself."

Rather than looking at his own memory of the information, Theodore wanted to blank-slate it: Read up on the current science without bringing his own education into it as anything other than a tool. It was a trick he'd learned in battle practice, pretending not to know what you knew so you'd be more aware of the specifics of what happened. That universal tendency to fill in the blanks no matter how little, or how much, information was applicable or available.

The Link processed First Contact the way it did viruses: By sandboxing unfamiliar code before it ever entered the processing centers of the brain, then using outsourced and downtime processors in the unconscious levels to analyze and decrypt it. These strictures and protocols were the strongest things in the Union; they had to be, people weren't naturally given to trusting brain implants in the first place, but again: After some tragedies, it just wasn't pragmatic to trust the brain's self-healing and self-regulating properties. People could, and did, try some very sick things.

So you have a community, say, of these people or whatever they were, traveling around the galaxy trying to get people onboard with their upload. Synthetic or somehow evolved that way, it didn't really matter. This could have been going on for a year or ten thousand years, depending on the culture of origin. But they wouldn't have been able to proliferate until the Link, probably, so under a hundred years of real colonization.

Maybe it wasn't even Outriding's great parabolic ears that picked them up, either. Maybe they'd hitchhiked to her, across the stars, looking for depot. Looking for a home. And everywhere they went, every mind they touched, either locked down before the person was conscious of it, or accepted the deal. And those that fell into a mind that recognized it as a virus, they were slaughtered. Forever forgotten. Crushed out by those same cold equations that kept you from choking on advertising every time you checked an email.

All of those souls.

He hopped to it, before Outriding could react. Opened a screen and started shouting.

"Shen4yla I fxxxxgured it out + I wont say a5ythhhhng but wehave to STOP.it now. Before a6yb6dy esl gets hurt. Th3m OR us."

She nodded, and shut down the lab to all outside noise so he and Outriding could come and stand with her, undetected.

"Th8y ARRRRRRR us."

Shen closed her eyes, ashamed, and nodded again.

*

"Tell her I can handle it. I know this is about me, I know it's something obvious that I can't see. Whatever it is, tell her I'll be okay. She thinks I'm stupid because of the way I talk, but she'll trust you."

Theodore didn't love that idea. Shen seemed pretty jealous of her relationship with the AI; he didn't want be translating for them, get between it. She'd make assumptions he didn't want made, and since he wouldn't make any more sense than Outriding, she'd have no choice but to get defensive with poor Theodore, wherever he was.

But she was right. He waited for Outriding to give him the words, and then he said them as carefully as he could.

"Otriding s4y:: sw3et lady, lovelady. :: trust me2b STRON8 as you made me. S4ys:: Strong az uuuuuuu ar."

Shen cried dry tears, clutching at her face. One hand snatched claws at her belly: The seat of both mind and emotion, for the dead people that raised her. Her heart.

"Outriding, I don't like any part of this. I don't want you to see me afraid. Or this guy. I don't want to *be* afraid. Face-to-sky. I wanted to be brave. And if you remember—*when* you remember—you're going to remember all of it. You're going to remember how bad it has gotten. How bad it's going to get. You don't..."

Outriding put one arm on Shen's chest, drawing close. Like a daughter, or a sister; waving a hand near her face so Shen would look up.

"itz wh4t he said,,, though. Strong as u made me/and i can b. 4u. just y lie."

"Honestly? I thought you would go rat-in-drum. I thought we couldn't have two crises on the station at the same time. I didn't understand at that point they were linked, or I would have done it differently. I would have done a lot differently. But I was already stacking-the-stones against you knowing the situation when they first made the offer. And I just couldn't. It would not be rock-on-sand, it wouldn't be real. If you didn't know, then nobody would know. I would be... *I don't have any family*," Shen said suddenly, whirling around on Theodore.

"I do not have friends. I do not have a culture. I am Outriding, but that is *all* that I am. Even here I am out-of-antumbra. But I have her, I understand her. And she... tolerates me."

Outriding shook her head angrily, pranking about until Shen breathed again.

"...And she could be so good, Theodore. She could be so bright. And I can *do* that. I can spend the rest of my life, however brief it is, on that. Bringing her back online, putting her back together. It is why I wanted you. I would have broken a lot more fingers to get you. Because there is just... not a lot of time."

Shen was disgusted at him for knowing it. That much was clear from her twisting face. But that was nothing compared to the comfort she was feeling, getting it all out. Letting Outriding hear it, without forgetting it. Making it real. He didn't want to throw her off more with that glitchy dumb speech, but he didn't know what else to do. He set his lips firmly and affirmatively, hopefully demonstrating his respect. A wounded soldier wouldn't want your pity, they'd want this.

"I did not mean for anyone to die. I thought they were safe once they got on-station. From my time with the People I neurologically am... I do not dream. We sift-the-world, an active process. Apparently I was young enough that I adapted, so now I do this instead of dropping into REM. I barely sleep at all, but when I do I fall like a... This does not matter. The point is that I could be mindful of them but keep the cordon, uniquely as far as I know. Until you came, and we could use you as the face-of-war. Stalking horse. Any further would mean killing more of them, or tying up Outriding's mind even more than I already am. I was trapped."

Outriding blinked out, sending Shen's eyes wide, but Theodore gave her a tiny nod: Outriding was losing it, all right, but that was no reason to upset Shen further. Not when she could spend that energy on picking apart all those lost moments and memories. He didn't want to see, but he hoped it was good. He hoped they'd cried when he wasn't there. Or done whatever they needed to do, before. What now they would have always done.

"I was drawn to it, and repulsed by it, because they were all in their last-walk-home. I cannot conceive of myself this way. So I began to learn their stories, like the stories of the People. To put them into my body, the way I did the elders. So that they would live-in-song, remembered. That was how I met the... They are of many races, you know. They have taught one another words even harder to translate than the People had. They have a name for themselves but I cannot say it."

They rapped at his digital skull, harder than ever. Begging to come in.

"It would be almost forty thousand words long. The simplest translation would be E=MC2 but even that leaves out most of the twists in the story, most of the contexts. Probably somewhere in there is an indication of where they came from, how old they are. I do not much care about that either. Their story is irrelevant. I only know they come for me soon, and you..."

Today. If Theodore agreed, he would be dying today.

And if he didn't? Was this not the purpose of his creation? To find a way to save this race, and this station; to fill him up with knowledge and language and be done.

"m3333 t0day. Yes. Yes."

Shen nodded, with something that might have been respect.

"I'll get started. Outriding, tell the Mockingbirds they can stop looking for Theodore Castelline. I'm the Contactee, he doesn't know anything. They can bring him here..."

She looked back over her shoulder at Theodore from the console with a questioning look, and he shook his head.

"Don't bring him here. Just take him home. Let him rest and take him home."

Outriding popped up a realtime screen for her in response, unbidden, and Theodore peeked over her shoulder: Theodore sitting in the sunny Hinge with his back against the fountain, as a small gaggle of gigantic thugs closed in on him, guns at the ready.

Shen began to laugh, and beckoned him closer to the screen. Putting one finger to her lips, she nodded and pointed at the leader, zooming in. Theodore gasped.

The metadata around the villain didn't match the face, at all. It was like looking at two people at once: One an enemy, the other something only a little less terrifying.

"That's Fairfax *Rapparee*, the famous *highwayman*," Shen explained, deadpan. "You can tell by his Link, which tells us his name. And his many great crimes."

She opened another screen, zooming in realtime on infrared again: You could just make out the shadow inside Greener's skull where his two Links sat, nestled side by side.

"Theodore will be fine. Safe-between-arms. Do you see what I am saying?"

Theodore nodded, relieved. As embarrassing as they both found Bobby's playacting—or whatever it was that they were looking at now—at least his other self had been found, and in one piece.

*

Bobby shook his head at Theodore, even when they were alone, quicker than a shot. He put his back against the door and sagged—for the moment's breath before he was sure they were locked down—and then abruptly breaking into laughter.

"You weren't supposed to see that. Him. Oh my God."

"What the hell, Bobby."

Bobby pointed at his face, giggling. He rolled his eyes, clearly much too keyed up to make much sense.

"I got a second Link installed several years ago. It throws up a few different personae, depending on what needs to get done. When I'm down here, it's usually to soothe some upset mob boss's hurt feelings, or take down a lunatic, so it has the most cover. Most of them are only names and histories, barely any cover at all. Frankly I don't even dress up for those. But Fairfax, he needs a little flair."

"I'm looking right at you, Bobby. You look like Bobby."

"To you, yeah. You're *blind*. It would take a lot more to fool you. But these guys, they see my kill ratio, or I mean Fairfax's, and look at my med stats, and never even go near my face."

Theodore was physically ill. That wasn't just criminal, it was seditious.

"Don't look at me like that, Castelline. I know who I am. I know what I'm doing. And the second I go corrupt, you can go ahead and cuff me, I won't complain. But do I really need to break the news to you that EADC has a Special Ops office? One of the largest intelligence clinics in the Commonwealth? What do you think those guys do, exactly?"

"Data analysis, AWOL trackers..."

"Corporate espionage, illegal extractions, kidnappings, assassinations..."

"Not EADC. That's just sensationalism. Competitor propo."

Bobby cast Theodore a look, worried he'd gone too far. Like he was some kind of innocent.

"You don't have to worry about hurting my feelings, Greener. I love EADC because I love it, not because I need it. And I'm telling you: Not EADC. When an enemy attacks your reputation, the master shows an open hand. They bring filth only upon themselves, and the master remains clean."

"Chapter and verse," Bobby sighed, disgruntled. Mentally checking off some new box next to Theodore's name. He needed to change the subject, urgently. If Bobby was going to get defensive about this Fairfax character he played, enough to go after a sore spot like the EADC no less, it served nothing to pursue it now. But the Captain would need to be notified.

Two Links in a single mind, sending out lies: That was worse than the ugly shirts. Not just ghosts from a children's nightmare, but actual demons. He didn't like to see Bobby that way. And it certainly didn't fit into his plans for secondary study. Those were not the white-hat kind of social engineering skills he needed to learn. Those were black arts.

"Thank you for saving me, Bobby. I mean that. I was afraid, and lost. Very hungry. I knew you'd come."

"...You know *I* would come? Specifically?"

Theodore snorted, in a way he hoped seemed genuine.

"I certainly wasn't expecting *Dexter*."

THE MISSING MAN

OUTRIDING

BY JACOB CLIFTON

PART FOUR

Chapter Ten: Some Grudges Remained

"They're calling it," Bobby Greener said, looking up and to the left. The game was over. Theodore could go home, finally, and settle into his new life.

By the set of Bobby's mouth, cruel, and his brow, cocked, it was clear he was still in Fairfax Rapparee mode: His alternate persona, connected to the station Hub through a secret secondary Link implant. That meant he was hearing it on the news, rather than from one of their crewmates. Could that be trusted?

"We're going to come up against a few... We're not done playing pretend, Castelline. I can't just walk you to Admin, the Mockingbirds are already on alert and my own guys would probably kill me just for the stats. I am not your friend."

True enough. Theodore hated Fairfax, he decided. Which must have showed: Fairfax jumped, a little startled. Perhaps even wounded. The slight squint magnified, as if taking the hit for the rest of his face.

"...Wow. I mean, I know you don't like the persona but... We're doing this to help you. Save you. Remember that part?"

"That isn't exactly true either. Let's get this over with. How do you get me back out there without being seen? I can't just escape, that would embarrass you. So what is it? Remand me over to the Mockingbirds? They won't be tricked by your little show, they'll know who you are. They'll take down Fairfax and the Captain will have to censure you for breaking Commonwealth and Union law.

Which will happen anyway, if I have anything to say about it. So what does that leave?"

Bobby shook his head, surprised at Theodore's nastiness. "Castelline, not twenty-four hours ago I sat on your bed and took care of you. I thought we..."

"—*That* was Bobby Greener. He's my friend. You are nothing to me. You're a repulsive criminal and I hate... I hate that you exist."

It wasn't just knowing Bobby was carrying demons in his head, or how deeply that struck at the transparency of the world. If you could be multiple people that was worse than being nobody. It was a nightmare, like finishing a novel and then finding out you'd gone aphasic halfway through, finding only pages of gibberish instead. It was like finding out your currency, your children's' futures, were underwritten by swiftly rotting vegetables, or slavery. The utter disconnect, between the solid world and the floating image... And Bobby thought this was funny?

But that wasn't the worst part. The worst part was that Bobby Greener and Fairfax Rapparee *were* different men. They stood different, talked different. Smelled different. It was grotesque. If your body, every signal it was sending to Theodore's blinded eyes, could change so drastically between personae—if Fairfax were just a software program, then so was Bobby. And then so was Theodore, too. And their bodies were just stinking puppets, hideously brought to life by any number of... It *was* repulsive, that was the word. There was no reason for an abomination like this to exist. Knowing it did made the universe a worse place.

Fairfax nodded, growing hard again. "That's valid. But if you think for a second the Captain doesn't value Fairfax over Bobby Greener, you have a very naïve concept of leadership. Please just stop... Talking, until I can get rid of you, okay?"

Now that sounded like Bobby. Theodore almost smiled.

"How much of you is different? I need to know. If you put two brainscans up alongside each other, you and Bobby..."

Fairfax nodded. "80 or so. 90% when Fairfax started, but we've deviated since then."

So they shared a body, and all the same memories, but... Fairfax was a choice. A deliberate choice, to be disgusting.

"How many of you are there?"

"Installed? Four others. But Castelline, please don't think about this right now. I can tell it's making you sick and I'm... Still me. Mostly. And it's not like being mean to me isn't also being mean to Bobby, okay? Because I'll be honest, everything in my body is telling me to coldcock you. That's what Fairfax would do to a hostage. You have to take it easy."

"Do you... Talk to each other? Do you have conversations?"

He felt like he was going to vomit for sure, now. Behind Bobby's face, a jail cell full of monsters.

"It's really not like that, okay? Now we just... This situation isn't tenable. Being here, with you, acting like this, it's inducing too much stress on the... You could actually damage my wetworks with this. Avoid me from here on out."

"Gladly," Theodore hissed, and Fairfax laughed. He jerked Theodore roughly to his feet, tying his hands behind his back, but not roughly. In fact, not tightly at all.

"Keep those on until we run into Karnides, okay? It has to look real. There's a swarm, uh... directly outside. When I open this door, that's it. We don't know each other. And I'm sorry."

It was bright outside the thieves' den; Theodore blinked there a moment before Fairfax shoved him, hard, in the center of the back, and he stumbled forward.

*

Fairfax kept up a running patter with his boys as they walked back into the center quad of the Hinge, but Theodore was tired of listening. Mercs and soldiers talk about different things. It was crude, to start with, and they were so rude to each other. It wasn't even about letting off stress, or bonding, or any of that. They were simply low.

Theodore kept his eyes high and his hands grasping one another, high on his back, praying they wouldn't try to include him in their conversation. He supposed he could take it from Fairfax, but if one of these brutish idiots got into the mood to tease him, that would end up with his face in the dirt. He knew that much. But they took even less notice of him than he did them, and that was probably best too. They focused on Fairfax to the exclusion, almost, of one another.

He didn't suppose he was really acquitting himself very well. Just because Fairfax was the closest thing to a monster he could conceive, that didn't excuse his prim behavior. Even now, among these men and women—his people—he had his nose in the air. They were disgusting, but that didn't mean he needed to be. Theodore resolved to just be angry, to brood, to throw them mean looks when possible, and just trust that Fairfax would keep him safe from reprisal.

Eventually they made their way, eight strong, to a makeshift barracks bar just sunside of the fountain where they'd picked him up.

The mercs shoved him into a chair and then surrounded him, discussing what they'd do with their shares of his ransom. Given what Fairfax had said about his usefulness to the Captain, Theodore was sure there was a slush fund for his criminal activities, paid for out of Outriding, which was upsetting.

But not as upsetting as the suspicion that Fairfax must have, at some point, earned these mercs' respect. How would that be arranged? Given the amount of detail put into the current game Outriding's crew were playing, it seemed possible that was pretty baroque. But Greener, at least, was in favor of simplicity and directness, in plans and conversation; Theodore figured he must have done some pretty bad things, as Fairfax. Maybe bad enough that turning back into Bobby Greener was its own reward.

As much as he hated it, he was fairly fascinated by this. It was easier to tune them out this way, anyhow. Karnides would know, although whether the old thing would tell or not, Theodore couldn't say. He couldn't quite imagine Bobby doing anything terrible, not really. Not even as Fairfax. The way he'd described it, he was almost a superhero, swinging into the Hinges when villains needed putting down. But that couldn't be the whole story, could it? Perhaps the mercs were weekend warriors, too; maybe this was all playacting.

It was only when Theodore reminded himself not to create facts out of nowhere *again* that he realized he was getting used to blindness. Online, he would be looking at a timeline of Fairfax's exploits, stem to stern, and figuring out exactly when he'd sprung into existence. Instead, blind, he was sitting in the middle of what seemed to be ramping up towards a barfight, running scenarios.

He didn't like it. He didn't like the idea of ever getting used to this invisibility, this loneliness. You could just eat yourself up that way. Just entirely devour yourself.

*

Karnides sloped into the room, grumbling, and things got a little quieter. He signaled to the bartender, two fingers straight up, and apparently the guy knew what that meant. From the hushed talk at his immediate elbow, Theodore was able to glean that Karnides was a known quantity: Dour, scary, Admin but somehow allowed into the rougher areas unmolested. Maybe they all just liked him as much as Theodore did. Karnides sat a few tables away, alone, and sipped his drink without meeting Theodore's eyes. This time, he caught himself before the spiral: No, you're not being abandoned. This is just part of the game.

Fairfax tapped him lightly under the table, jutting a chin in Karnides' direction.

"You see that old wolf?"

Theodore nodded in as hateful a fashion as he could manage; under the table, Fairfax squeezed his knee supportively.

"Get up and walk over there, bring me back a package. Slow, so we can watch."

Some of the rougher mercs whistled, just a little bit, but it died once Fairfax deigned to acknowledge them. Theodore angled up out of the chair, hoping his fake bonds would hold, and stumbled toward Karnides, who met him with a snarl and one rheumy eye. He clicked his tongue in disgust.

"Get yourself lost, boy? This comes out of your paycheck, you know that. Damn fool."

Theodore turned around, head hanging, and Karnides put the package—whatever it was—in his bound hands. The hooting was louder this time, as he picked his way between the creeps. Their legs seemed to have doubled, in number and length, for the return trip.

When he stood before Fairfax Rapparee, the man's squint redoubled, and he jerked his chin again.

One hand braced gently on his back, Fairfax cut Theodore's bonds with the other, and set the package on the chair, under one thigh. He snickered and reached out to pat Theodore's face with one open hand.

"Good doing business with you, librarian. Call me," he added, in a high voice that sent the guys off again. The women in the company seemed just about as tired of this performance as Theodore was, but the men were like hyenas, laughing and climbing all over one another. It was hard to love them, that was for sure. But at least he hadn't blown Bobby's cover. He never could have forgiven himself for that.

Not until he was back home, at least.

*

A block past the exit, Karnides exhaled loudly, putting his arm lightly through Theodore's as if they were on a casual stroll. A boy and his grandfather, perhaps; that white stripe in the black hair. His pet werewolf, with the gold ring in his ear.

"I'd be blind, if I could. Don't much guess that helps you, though. Probably excited to get back to it."

That wasn't exactly what he was feeling, but Theodore agreed with the gist of the sentiment. He wanted to give Karnides something in return.

"They wouldn't let me talk to you. I kept asking for you but they said..."

"—Don't much trust their plans, either. But they kept you safe, didn't they."

They walked. The stitching on Karnides' uniform was hidden cunningly enough, but up close you could see just how jagged the tailoring had to be, to pull his warped body together as well as it did. The strange bent angles. Theodore wondered, not for the first time, if the old man were in pain. He walked heavily, as though everything hurt, but that could just be how he walked.

Blind, his face was even more fascinating: Scarred, pulled in different directions almost horribly, but somehow calm and comforting for all that. Rogue hairs, a twisted mouth that nonetheless did not betray his speech. He must work hard at that too, Theodore thought. And all this time, with that muscled arm wrapped around Theodore's own, making it seem so tiny; holding him together as they walked the long way home.

*

"You're safe in quarters. Mockingbirds posted outside, as they said before. Crew's on Link congratulating you, even though they know you can't hear it."

Karnides closed the door behind them, shutting down surveillance as though Theodore were about to break into tears or screams.

"You watch out for that Bobby Greener. He's beside himself and liable to start shouting. I don't know what you said to Fairfax but it's got him all twisted up."

Theodore nodded. That wasn't going to be a pretty reunion.

"Outriding too. Just take a shower and try to relax. Your part's almost finished. It's up to him now."

The other Theodore. He hadn't thought of him all day.

"Is he okay? Have you talked to him?"

Karnides shook his head, quickly.

"No thanks. But I hear they're getting along like old friends, that one and Outriding."

"How developed is he? I mean, is he a... Does he have any reactions? Is he just a program or..."

"Shen says he's just like you. Talks like Outriding, otherwise true."

That wasn't what they'd promised. They had said he'd be a barebones thing, a computer virus version of himself. He didn't want to think about that other one suffering, if he was anything approaching a real AI.

"Can I see him? Talk to him, when it's done?"

Karnides listened.

"Says maybe. He wants to meet you too. Could be a moment, five minutes maybe Shen says. Before he's gone."

Whatever that meant. Theodore supposed there was a chance he could hang around, somehow. If Outriding liked him, that made Theodore happy. She seemed a little lonely. Especially now, he supposed, she would be.

"Does Outriding know about Shen? Does anybody?"

Karnides nodded. "Yesterday we didn't. I suppose the Captain's Second did. Perhaps Lorna Sciorro. But now we do. And I believe

Outriding does. There were some minor outages, but it seems the other Theodore helped, somehow. They aren't talking about it."

Some bit of Karnides, one corner of his back, told Theodore further questions wouldn't be welcome. Perhaps Shen herself didn't know the details. It seemed possible that with her altered physiology they might have no name for what she was going through.

Far back in the annals of the Union, some races had found an exuberance in the discovery of spaceflight that led to some pretty awful things. If you don't recognize a race as sentient, you can do all kinds of things in the name of science that later generations might find less than ethical. The greater part of First Contact protocol was devoted to underscoring and eliminating these trespasses, in one way or another: Not that they would hurt us, but that we would somehow hurt them, before we found out they were people.

The Commonwealth of human worlds had a hard time swallowing it, but one of the central tenets of First Contact history was about treating those races who had so trespassed, in the past, with decency. The assumption of evil or conquest was something humanity was not allowed to bring with it: Like any historical horror, it was important in Union to recognize those monstrosities as mistakes, never to be repeated, but surely not to be punished forever. Some grudges remained, of course, but they were acknowledged and transparent: The point was not fairness, or even justice, but simply the knowledge that these acts must not be repeated, and rooting out what influence they had on the future.

The young Earth particularly, having been visited over a few late centuries before uplift by some of these rogue races—and with its own historical genocides and imperialism still fresh—pantomimed agreement, but dig a little deeper and you'd still see some paranoia, written blood-deep. And this too was understood and welcomed by the Union, as they'd seen it a hundred times before.

It was a process, they'd been taught, and although EADC was in some ways fairly hidebound this was one aspect of uplift they recognized more easily than others. A military corporation had, perhaps, a unique vantage on this particular form history could take: The shifting allegiances, the apologies so great that words cannot contain them. The million ways we have made to find recompense, balance, hope for redemption.

And so part of what made the thrilling, tragic story of Shenayla B'Coreneis so captivating to the Commonwealth, and to Earth particularly, was just this physical transformation that seemed to be destroying her now: Although they'd been her rescuers and fostered her as an orphan, they'd changed her no less dramatically than those old flying-saucer monsters in the stories did their victims.

Like humanity she was welcomed, taken in, by alien life; like humanity she was changed utterly by it. Her brief career as a terrorist, even, was touted as the ultimate expression of human values: She fought a corrupt system, and won. How could any son or daughter of the Commonwealth do less?

For the first time, Theodore saw Shen the way he thought Dexter did, maybe even Outriding herself: She wasn't just a weird bitch, or a traitor hiding up in the Core while the population burned. She was a symbol of hope, synergy between an upstart race and the greater Union. It wasn't something anyone would verbalize, and it would be intensely disrespectful if one did, but the truth remained that Shen was, even in her backwater third career where nobody could see her anymore, even as it faded, a celebrity: Her body was for them a marriage, not a battleground.

Dexter had seen combat, during his adventures; of them all he'd be most likely to hold onto those old fights. But he was more dedicated to Outriding's mission than any of them. Or at least louder about it. So if there was something wrong inside Shen, if that marriage of the solar system and the Rim was tainted—if the transplant didn't take—

where did that leave Bryce? Where did it leave any of them? And what the hell would they do when she was gone?

*

Bobby was Bobby, when he returned. Even blind, Theodore could see that. He hated the shame in Greener's eyes at the door, but didn't know how to fend it off. They weren't friends, he couldn't take the guy into a rough embrace, the way they did in stories. He still felt a little too uncanny, somewhere back inside Theodore, to completely relax. But he knew Bobby felt strongly about their contretemps, and there needed to be something to mark it. To move on.

How to begin. Always, that. And like always, Theodore let the other guy lead.

"You made me feel disgusting."

Theodore shook his head, as if committing to a pretense: *What do you mean? My old friend, my old pal and Social Director Mr. Greener, what on Earth could you possibly.*

"I mean that I just... The way you looked at me, Theodore, it floored me. Even through the other guy. Don't say his name, it'll flag," he waved tiredly, knowing Theodore would probably start mumbling if he didn't.

"A lot of the emotional energy doesn't... It's mostly like a film, like I remember watching it and feeling sad. So I'm not still angry at you or anything. But it's been hard to go back to look at myself the way I used to. I guess I just never thought about it from your perspective. Somebody that grew up like you did, looking at me like I was nothing. Like I was filth. It just really..."

Theodore twitched, head to toe. So anxious he felt light-headed. And still, no words.

"I don't want you to apologize or anything. I guess I just wanted you to know that. I wasn't—he wasn't either—making fun of you, or your beliefs, or... Whatever. Your complaint is registered, okay? I'm not going to stop doing it, it keeps everyone on this station safe. But I won't be able to forget how it made you react. It made me feel... Like when you're young, and you think everything is easy and safe and happy, and then one day another kid steals from you, or slaps you or something, and you just have to adjust to a world with those things in it. Now we know something about each other, and it's not great, but we *live* there now. So I'm sorry that I came at you on the EADC stuff. I don't think either of us did anything wrong, but I do feel bad about reacting. What you did was instinct, it was healthy. What I did back was just hurt feelings, and that's very embarrassing. Okay?"

Bobby finally looked up, into Theodore's mystified eyes, and snorted that laugh again.

"...And I can tell I'm just making it worse, so all right. All right, Theodore. You win. God."

A good bit of the Fairfax squint stole over Greener, for a moment. Like he was trying to find Theodore's weak points, without showing it, for a sudden assault. But it never came.

"No. Bobby, no. I won't apologize and I can't say it's okay. It's a betrayal of everything you, and this station, and our entire Commonwealth stand on. And I know that you know that. But please don't think I'm going to be thinking about you, or that I care..."

Bobby grimaced, rubbing the back of his head, and stepped toward the door without a word.

"No, Bobby. Oh man. No, see this is why I don't talk. Um, what I was going to say is that I am a soldier and you don't know very many soldiers and I never saw combat but this—thing you have going on, inside you, it's—gross. It's immoral, it's a sin, okay. Unforgiveable."

Bobby nodded, hips slung sideways, like he was getting bored. Bottom lip sticking out just a little bit, in a pout. Even his hair seemed offended.

"But Bobby, so is killing. So is hurting people, and forcibly... We move populations around that don't want to move, we make very hard choices on a mass scale, and we hurt people and we kill them, for the Corps and for the Commonwealth. We take on that burden for the people we serve. You think the sacrifice is about getting shot at, but it's not. That's a job hazard but it's not why we pray, or why we serve, or... The sacrifice is getting your hands dirty so somebody else's get to stay clean. That's what a soldier is: Not the guy who gets shot at, but the guy who *shoots*. That's why we fight. That's *how* we serve."

Theodore breathed, then, finally, and looked at the floor. He knew they weren't, but he didn't want to know for sure whether those really were tears in Bobby's eyes, after all. It was enough to know he'd said it, and that Bobby was hearing him.

"So if you tell me that this is necessary and you tell me that you don't get off on it, that you know why it is gross, then who am I? Who am I to tell you anything about it? You don't know me well enough for us to be talking about this but certainly you do not know me well enough to presume that I would ever judge you. Or even what I think about you, or any of this. Not yet. Not when I'm just so recently blinded, and we've just met. You saw me under a lot of pressure and you cut corners you didn't need to, to make sure I wasn't *just* safe, but so I wouldn't lose my mind, okay? So I wouldn't lose my *shit*. I saw you doing that. I won't tell anybody. But I did see it."

From the corner of his eye, still downcast, Theodore saw the blur of Bobby drop his head, deeply, chin to chest, like a salute to something fallen. And then he was shuffling backwards, again. And then he was gone.

*

When Bryce Dexter came to bring Theodore to Core, by his request, there was a falsity, an exhaustion, to his heartiness that Theodore was starting to think was only ever a matter of degree. How much energy, how many *calories*, must it take to be Bryce Dexter? To keep that act up? The number seemed infinite.

"Mr. Dexter. Sir. If we have a moment, I just wanted to thank you for your help over the past few days. I know you're a very busy man and I wasn't the easiest prisoner to... Your kindness and empathy were an unexpected comfort during all of this. You have gone above and beyond your duty in this matter, and it seems to me, from what I have seen and heard, that this is typical both of your service and your character."

He saluted, hoping his little prepared speech didn't sound as unctuous as it suddenly did now, echoing in his ears, and finally chanced a look at Bryce when no answer was forthcoming. He seemed hollowed out. Was it Shen? Had something happened to Shen? What was the next calamity?

"I don't know what you—at ease, Castelline, we don't do that here—I don't know what you pulled on Green but he's a mess. And I think it's probably a good mess, nobody needs a shakeup more than that kid, but I want to be very clear about what exactly will happen to you if you play with him."

Theodore was shocked, but Bryce Dexter held out one giant hand nearly in a fist, to keep him quiet and still.

"On the off chance that you have come here with the intention of playing any emotional games with staff, I will recommend you for treatment, okay. I will get EADC in here to run mods on you so fast and hard you'll be clockworked before you ever start work. This isn't the Corps, you have a lot of behavioral leeway—if you've met Shen you already know this—but intentionally screwing around with the Social Director of the largest diplomatic craft in known space is something that will really endanger your position here. Clear?"

Theodore nodded, back still quite straight.

"Permission to freek speely? Speak freely? Sir?"

Dexter didn't move.

"I am getting really tired of you guys telling me what to do, if we're being honest. At the risk of insubordination, sir, I'm sick of it. Sick as hell. I don't know what your preoccupation is with Greener, and as I said before I'm very grateful for your kindness, but this circle-the-wagons game you guys play with each other... Now, and I'm sure it makes you feel just great. I'm sure it's *great* for morale. But you keep telling me I'm part of the team and then you come in here on absolutely the worst day of life with random threats about shit you cannot possibly know about or understand, that sends a mixed message. Here on the largest *diplomatic craft* in known space."

"...Valid."

"Do you know how I got back to quarters? Do you know the hell that was? Do you know I was taken into custody by a mercenary in the Hinges? Do you know the particular one I am talking about?"

It began to dawn on Dexter what Theodore was saying, and he pulled his lips back in a silent *yee*, but Theodore was not quite finished.

"The foundation of the Union, Mr. Dexter, is nationality without locality. Life beyond location, nation beyond soil. And the underpinning of that, all across the civilized worlds, the thing that keeps our glorious syndicates running, is the Link. That's sacrosanct, sir. Identity itself. Citizenship. At least how I was brought up. So please do forgive me if I try to hang onto to just one of my beliefs. Just one little piece of home, before I join this team you're so excited about defending."

Bryce wobbled his head all around, in a sort of apologetic funk. Even with that hangdog look he affected, that sheepish L'il Green hunger he sometimes got, he still looked like the movies. Lantern jaw, chiseled cheeks, twinkling eyes. Silly old overbearing blustering sputtering Bryce Dexter, built like an ox, looking for all the world like he'd got caught with the last of the muffins. It was maddening, but it was also deadly effective. No wonder everybody, even Bobby, indulged him so much.

"That'd do it. I hear you, son. I apologize. I didn't know you'd, ah, run into that member of the population."

"Okay then. Are we good?"

The Captain's Second broke out in a radiant smile, relieved. For a grizzled old soldier, even a comic-book hero version of one, he didn't seem to enjoy conflict much.

"Well, now you know. We protect our own, and that gets fierce when it needs to. And you're right, that includes you. So the next time you think somebody's going over your head, remember who's watching out for you."

Theodore pretended to find that as reassuring as Bryce Dexter clearly wanted him to, and they headed Coreward.

Chapter Eleven: Scrape-The-Sun

The young Theodore they brought to visit, on the last day of his life, was a nervous sort.

From what they'd said, the footage he'd reviewed, Theodore knew he'd been through a lot. Only after the Fairfax kidnapping—when the kid knew for certain that he was safe—had it gotten really bad. Limbic system stayed pretty even, with some spikes, until then. He didn't feel the danger until he was safe, that was part of it: Delayed shock.

But for Theodore, it was clear what really bothered him was learning he couldn't trust Bobby anymore, because that brought the whole thing down: If the rest of them did, then they were all enemies too. When Shen showed him the double-implant that brought Fairfax to life, part of it was humor and relief, but part of him knew Theodore wouldn't respond well.

He'd balked at speaking to this boy in Outriding's glitchy tongue, but they'd offered to bring him in, rather than sending Theodore out. He liked that idea a lot; getting to show himself around the station, in this strong new body. How much he'd love just that feeling, of holding all these people inside himself, breathing for them, making the sun shine. Keeping them safe.

As long as he remained physically in the Core, they could hook the boy up to Outriding's system directly, without bothering with the Link, and he'd still be clean. The virus wouldn't see him, and the game could continue. He'd prove out, solving the problem and ending the experiment, and those souls would never have to risk death again, on any strange planet or in any stranger's mind. They could find the form they wanted.

If Theodore could work fast enough, creating a language for them the Link would recognize, they could formally accept First Contact and join the Union. Outriding, of course, agreed to sponsor them, with a unanimous vote. The families of the dead, once they'd understood what was at stake—where their loved ones were, now— were the first to agree. And with them came all Union.

He thought Theodore would enjoy that part, the work itself, but there was no way he could move fast enough. Theodore and Outriding could move between moments, but there was no way to bring that body's autonomic responses up to their speed. Even if he had the processing power, which was theoretically possible, the metabolic effects would be deadly. So they would spend a few moments, and then he would start spinning language—not even Outriding could be around for all of that, not with the risks involved—and then, all accomplished, that would be it. Eternity.

But for now, they could talk. He could twist time around for Theodore, make it dance. Show him memories, if he wanted, but Theodore knew he wouldn't. He would just want to see him, look into his eyes. Make a speech, probably. Before leaving the City of Earth, goodbye wasn't a word in their vocabulary; now it was crucial.

**

"So you know it all now."

Outriding nodded, unwilling to speak. She was recording, for later. There were no more secrets anymore, and she knew if Shen wanted to confess it would come out all in a burst. She'd let Outriding sort it out, finally, instead of trying to control everything. Shen was a good friend, but a chronically worried one.

Shen sucked from a waterpipe, taking a sip of tea. Her joy lay in private affectations the crew, even Lorna Sciorro, didn't know about. She half-lay curled against the wall in her little Lab bunker, where she slept most nights, all her favorite secrets spread out around her. Pleasures of the body, mostly; some bitter tastes or harsh vapors, some sweet, some lately more poisonous.

It pleased her to go out among the population, not just the Hinges but the rings, in a little bit of a disguise. She was not so allergic to her celebrity that it bothered her when people recognized her, although part of the experience was, for them, to be rebuffed. She felt sometimes like a character from an old Earth theme park, an evil queen or an angry princess: Playing the role, making children squeal. Mostly people felt like they knew her, and spoke just so, which didn't much bother her either: Mostly, people did.

"Outriding. Would it be presumptuous to ask for a little poetry at my funeral? Some impassioned Yeats? Do not answer yet."

She read it aloud, despite the screen. Made it almost halfway through before her voice broke. It had been doing that lately, obnoxiously. Another betrayal. Outriding didn't mind when she talked about herself, but she hated doing it.

"*...What could have made her peaceful with a mind / That nobleness made simple as a fire...*"

Eventually, she finished. Outriding never seemed to care about emotional outbursts, even as she had her own. Maybe that was why she didn't.

"And so now I will ask you again: Is that too much? I am not even Irish, Sumpter is English. And I do not want it to be about my history, symbolic of the *song-of-fire*, all that terror. I just always thought somebody would read that for me, sometime."

"2 much naught enuffff. xoxo."

Shen was not a complicated person, really: Just intense. She was a simple woman in a complicated body, which was one level too many for most. The Sumpter-Fernandez clan was not known for peacefulness, even before the line ended. Ended on little Daisy, scooped up into chaos and pain and so much love, sifting the world. High, and solitary, and most stern. Less solitary now.

"It is... It will be him. Will it not. You know that now, you are certain."

The other Theodore was a test case in more ways than one. While Shen trusted Lorna Sciorro with almost anything having to do with their shared charge, it was the Librarian that would change things. If they could induce him to love Outriding even half as much as Shen did, he'd stick with her to the end. He'd rebuild her, from the inside out. It didn't matter if Shen liked him.

Not that she didn't, exactly. He was a kitten, something cute and easily destroyed, which bothered her. Megan Quire seemed to find him fascinating, which was a danger sign. The boys all fell right in line, though, as she'd known they would. For all his bluster Dexter was nothing before a pretty face, and Bobby couldn't have designed a more irksome personality for conflict with, even if he'd known that's what he wanted. And Karnides...

Well. You needed to keep Karnides busy, that's all. Before Theodore it was Salter he'd followed, like a dog. Whoever made him feel strongest, most peaceful; that's what kept the monster at bay.

"th1s 1 proves ittt. Oll korrect. My nu fri3nd."

Shen didn't like to think they depended on her. Especially not if they did, and didn't know it. She didn't like feeling above them, she hated leadership: Enough of that during the angry days. Enough of that for a lifetime, throwing her people—those young bodies, most of them still boys and girls—against the wall of corporate crap. Knowing they wouldn't all come home.

But it did make her feel safe, all those lines of power between her and the population. She knew Dexter and Bellar would keep everybody safe—but "everybody" is an approximation, always. There will always be exceptions, that's rule. She knew Karnides and even Salter and Bobby would do what they could to protect Outriding, which meant protecting her. That was a good number of bodies, to put between you and the black sky. And now this kid, who'd looked at her like...

Every time a ship docked, in the great starry expanse between Outriding's rings, and they'd crank open the great gates, part of Shen would dissolve in fear. The last remnants of Baby Daisy, somewhere far away and down in her, so far she could never quite sift enough to find her. If she dreamed, she supposed, one day she might meet that little girl again, and find just the right words to save her. Or drown her, whatever it took to kill the fear. But the People had taken that from her, too.

And so when the Med bay told her there wasn't a word for what was happening to her, no treatment for the thickening lesions along the medulla—at least, at first; when they first caught it—that biopsies proved you couldn't discern from basic carbon allotropes, once they were out. They found it in her colon, they found it in the joints of her ankles. They found it everywhere they looked for it, so she made them stop looking.

Diamond mind, decomposing swiftly into graphite, threatening stroke as it broke down further and further, silting into the bloodstream eventually. Irritants, growing pearls of illness around them as her body tried to understand and fight something it never should have known.

The People called it a gift. Perhaps even knew a cure. But they were gone now. Their line ended with her, too.

And so perhaps it was not Baby Daisy, down in the deeps, that shuddered every time a ship arrived. Maybe it was just her fear, a large thing blotting out the sun, that had found this one way to crack open the door, into her weakness. *Whoever is coming*, the knock said every time, *it is also me*. Her body, wanting to make sure she was in on the joke.

In any case, at some point in her years aboard it had stopped being about letting the others absorb the danger, and had started being about... Perhaps it was spending so much time with Outriding, who saw everything and was aware of everything inside herself. Perhaps it was a model she'd somehow begun to emulate; in her sift-the-world and civil meditations each night and morning, she'd begun to find it was easier to just imagine herself as the whole ship, the whole of Outriding, rather than one specific part. And somewhere around the time she admitted that, and committed to the process—feeling almost perverted, at first, for doing so—she realized she'd come to care about them, too. Her work with Outriding took on a different flavor then, but it went faster, too.

The boy had something of that in him, didn't he. Not just service, all of them had proven a hundred times over they had that, but that extra thing. The People called it turn-the-face; Dr. Sumpter would have called it "ego down," but it was certainly something she'd never been very good at, in practice. She doubted she could have survived any of the uncommon things she'd survived, if she didn't find herself to be pretty crucial. But this kid, it just rolled right off. A different kind of nobleness perhaps. Barely there, even in the digital version, but it was there. Outriding would need to work on that, when she was gone. She hoped he wouldn't be too angry.

Not that Outriding would care if he were; she was used to people resisting her. It was the natural response. But the boy seemed unpredictable: Didn't like being pushed around, so you had to manipulate him, but he seemed even more sensitive to that. The only thing he really seemed to take well was Bobby Greener's rudeness, and Shen's, so perhaps the direct route. Another thing Outriding was barely capable of, at this stage in her development. In her return to transcendence, as Shen and eventually Theodore alone would set those scarred bones aright, sometimes violently; the People's term was, for once, less precise: They called it *breaking-the-broken.*

There was always one, aboard. Taken sometimes from the dregs, or the Hinges—sometimes a very bad person indeed, which Outriding didn't remember directly but had left text logs about that were now (or at least *for* now) illegible—who held the keys. Not like a horse and her rider, exactly. Perhaps like a beekeeper with her bees, that's how Shen thought of it. EADC's own Theodore would want it in terms of the ancient laity: Not chaplain, but verger.

Theodore Castelline would want that, to be Outriding's verger. Easy call. But it meant Shen's time was up. The last task, and the most hateful, was vetting her successor. All this time she'd thought it was chosen for her by destiny, somehow, that she had been through all that shit and blood and pain and fire to make her special enough to keep these bees, and she found herself handing it over to the blandest little weenie she'd ever met in her life. Outriding was tough to take occasionally.

What Outriding wanted, and Shen refused to give her as long as they'd known each other, was to bring her into the Core: Even for only a second, to exist in the contiguous space. She would not ask. But she hinted.

To Shen it was a nasty thought: Not just drowning in her friend, which was perverse, and not just because the People would think so. But too, it would be hard seeing her become just like everybody else, and Shen didn't particularly *like* anybody else. And to be honest, she liked the glitch: It reminded her of home. All these reasons, and Outriding so ashamed to speak, always talking about how she used to be. As if that was helping. As if she could work faster, care more.

Even if today was the day, Shen decided, it wasn't a kindness she could spare. Uploading into the consciousness, whatever it decided to call itself, was an act of faith. To enact those sorts of rituals would be to admit she was frightened of what lay beyond. And that is not the sort of woman that Shenayla B'Coreneis had turned out to be, in the end.

*

"Hello? Am I? Hello? Is this it happening? Excuse me, I can't..."

Theodore waved a hand before the boy's face: His brain would be routing all this input through the neocortex, as though it were visual stimulation through the Link—much harder for a physical body to reconcile, if he spent too much time thinking about it.

"Treat it like a VR, okay? Like on the cryoliner. You're apt to hurt yourself if you act like it's an overlay. Hold your body very still until you can float here, like this. Leave your body there."

Theodore nodded, too preoccupied to acknowledge him yet, and focused his will on stretching out into the Core. He would have been blind all this time, maybe that would actually help. He smiled, raising one arm slowly; Theodore opened a screen to watch his brother's body, out in the Core lab. No movement.

"Good job."

The boy rolled his eyes at Theodore, smiling.

"Did you watch me like this when I was out there?"

"A little bit. We had to keep jumping. But I saw you with those mercs, when the flock almost caught up to you. To us."

"Is it true you talk like her, out there? I bet that sounds bizarre."

Theodore grinned ruefully. "You'd hate it. Trust me, you don't want to see that."

The boy held out his arms, then, and Theodore fell into them. It was strange, but good.

"Listen, I know we don't have a lot of time..."

Theodore leaned back, looking into his eyes. "That's just part of what is good here. It's not cut-and-paste, it's all copies. We can run time back, or forward, it's like..."

Theodore shook his head at that. "I hear you but I don't... That's your life, not mine. If I don't ever see you again I want to remember you this way, not like that. Not like an adventure. Just like this. Like friends."

"Okay. Tell me then, about your time on Outriding. I didn't see much. I didn't want to. But I would like to hear it from you."

He slowed time, not enough that Theodore would notice but enough that he'd have time to tell the story. And then, he did.

**

"Do you know the meaning of my name, Outriding? I know that you do. But I believe that I have never said aloud the story. Among the People. Maybe to anybody. I will not come in there with you, you may let go the burden of wishing for that. But I will tell you this."

Outriding put her hands on her hips, still not talking. Finally she nodded, only a little angry.

"We had these small mammals. Delicious. In Commonwealth they would look at you funny for eating them, much less the way we did. This animal, the warm-under-sand, was one of the few things that appealed to my sense of taste. The People ate not very often, but they ate a lot. So I ate not very often, and very little. I guess it was nutritious, I suffered from nothing in particular, although I did grow to be a skinny woman. That may be nutrition. But my metabolism, that is nothing to do with them. They left my gut alone for the most part."

Shen looked away and to the side, as she sometimes did with Outriding. Thinking about what was done to her, and how it kept her alive, and made her special. She knew that, even at the time: Her mother's *abuela* told her about the shamans, growing up: A long time ago, before anything really happened much, the witches would come into your tent, with the heads of animals, and they would take your body apart, and put you back together with a gem hidden away inside your skull. And after that you would know magic.

Her great-grandmother's point was that spirituality, for a serious little girl like Baby Daisy, was going to be an uphill battle: She would always be wondering where the shamans were, why they weren't putting things in her head. That they were real things. So she wanted to fill her up with stories, enough stories that she wouldn't ever have to wonder that. But instead, her family was murdered by greed, and she was taken in by men with the heads of animals, who told her that her heart was in her stomach and there were diamonds in her head. And now there were.

Daisy was sad and alone and hungry for a while, and she knew she had to hide from the rescue squads so they wouldn't get her too—it was the last thing her mother said—and then when the indigenes came, after that, and took her in, it all made sense. She was becoming magic. They nominally understood what this meant, and agreed with her, but she supposed they would have done it to her either way.

If Shen hadn't spoken up at the right times, shown the right skills and interests, they probably would have kept experimenting on her, the way her parents had studied them during the years of the expedition. But at some point they realized she—either born or built—had the sort of gifts that could be put to use. So they taught her their songs, and then the stories, and then the history, and then the things that underpinned it all.

Back in Commonwealth, when her corp was still pretending to look out for her, they studied her too. They were nice about it, just like the People; they didn't explain it, like the People did. They treated her more like a little mammal than the People ever had. And they said that most of it was bioengineering, and crude implants, but that some of the neurological damage—that was the word they used, "damage," as though what she could do was less interesting than what had been done—came from the songs and the stories and the histories and the truths of the People. They'd been rewriting her software as they rebuilt her hardware. And now look what they made.

It was only in the last year or so that Shen gave any thought to the idea that perhaps it wasn't the People's reprogramming at all, that was making her sick. Maybe whatever was broken happened when she got back. But there was nothing to do with those thoughts and feelings but sift them for gold, before bed, because all those helpful villains were dead and gone: Most of them she'd put the bullets into with her own hand. And it didn't matter anyway; what human science broke wasn't always what human science could fix.

You could only look so deeply into your own body, making up stories, before you realized it wasn't ever going to tell you a story back. Sometimes you knew why something was hurting, an injury or an infection; other times you could only visualize it, correctly or not quite, and that was as good as it got. No use it drawing that out. She'd put all those thoughts away a long time ago.

This is what it was to be Shen, the day they made First Contact: She wanted to know how she could preserve her brain matter, when her Link implant exploded. That's what she was doing, on her last day alive. Trying out scenarios—cryo, half-cryo, low-grav—that would preserve as much of her brain as possible when it caught fire. How quickly Outriding could put it out, and the safest way to do so.

"These small mammals, I did love them. The taste, and to feel them when they lived. When you are so young that you do not understand what you are seeing, you can watch something die and feel nothing. You grow, enough to understand what an ending is, and you make peace or you do not. You can never go backwards, Outriding. There is no return to innocence. Only more experience. But you will find an equilibrium, the closest you can be to when you were young. Where you understand that you will never care the way you did that first time. The first shock of death."

The People hinged a lot of early development around that moment, how you responded. It determined their caste, or what they in the Union called provenance: Another word was guild. Those who were able to eat-the-stone the fastest, who synthesized this mystery the fastest or the most calmly, were the warriors. The ones that never stopped eating it, they became doctors and scientists. Even builders, architects, because they knew how to protect life in a way that was so different from the warriors they said it was a different stone entirely that they were eating. And the ones that spit the stone out, those were the magicians, the healers and the singers.

"In the summer of which I speak there was a daily meteor shower in one corner of the sky that I knew meant they would soon ring the bell for evening meal. Our planet's orbit was... You know. It is how they died in the end. When they rang the bell I was heading home, already. I was almost a woman, however old that is for a human."

In those days Shen worked for four hours out in the crops, alone because nobody wanted to be around her, because she didn't want to be around anyone. And then she came home for studies, and was given an hour before dinner to roam the sands, which was her pleasure at that time.

"The People do not have a lot of visual components to their ritual. They were a race that put little emphasis on sight. There was a tone in everything they did that evening. And they were always testing me. If not about the adjustments, their gifts, it was about socializing me. They thought that I was wild, insane, and so they treated me as they would one of their own children who had gone wild. It got so that you could smell the difference."

Outriding reached out, guessing at the story, and Shen smiled at her. Something few beings in the galaxy had ever really seen. Beautiful.

"That day was special. I knew what death was of course. The evolved fauna on that planet had a ridiculously short lifespan and breeding cycle, most of them. This was the reason my parents brought us. I knew where my food came from. But to kill the food was a warrior's position. The population was already so sparse by that time it seemed like their only position. To kill so that the rest of us could eat without killing. But I felt on the wind that this night, I would be asked to kill."

There was a high incidence among the People of what Megan Quire would class with potlatch and similar societal token behaviors: In this case, a system through which each person would experience—once, but dramatically—the roles of the other castes.

"Even though I was no warrior, nor even doctor—you remember that I was practically a spiritual leader at this point, I was second from the top—it was important that we all taste the stones. All of them. How hard it was, to make war. Or if you were a warrior, how hard to hold back, to be still or quiet when you would speak. Whatever the thing you hate to do, you must do it, or you are not taking part in the world of... In other people. You would have no way of knowing in your body, in your center, what they carried with them. I understood this. I was preaching it, by then. I was surprised to find that it applied to me."

And within seconds, small delicious mammal in her hands, she broke open. Suppressed stress and trauma going back to that first day, she thought.

"Everything they taught—how to sift-the-world, sit in abeyance; how to hold-the-sky, all of it—just fell apart in me. I thought that they would exile me. Or kill me. Give me to the company that killed my parents."

She thought she was going mad, she thought she was becoming an angel. The People's autonomic systems evolved so differently from humans—from most sentient races—that concepts like fight-or-flight, even passion, had no real equivalents in their thought. No adrenals, no real concept of hormones. They were such easy pickings for Shen's nation of origin, they entered an almost hibernatory catatonia when startled. Bipeds with the mass of bison, falling over like possums whenever there was so much as a thunderstorm, and a one-word lexicon for the whole of adolescence: *Day-of-fire.*

"They have passion but it is a sustained activity, riding-on-swells, not an overwhelming. It is not passion but it serves the same purpose. On a schedule. My body was a timebomb. Everything within me, gratitude and love, desperation to belong: All of it said, you are coming apart. All of it said, this life of pretending to be something you are not. Living in the society and teachings developed around bodies as different from yours as the body of this little beast. This little terrified thing. Might as well ask her, to save them. To take their souls into her body, before she dies of fright and is dissected for your evening meal."

Outriding perched on the edge of the bed, excited for what would happen next.

"I fled into the mountains, dropped my little victim and ran. There was a cave, up one bluff, that I would use to watch them dance the wheel, when they would send me out of the city. And my spiritual mentor—an old, old thing that had borne many children before they took me in, none of whom had survived—clambered up along those rocks, making a sound that I associated with humor. It was so strange, I remember thinking for a moment that all of it, the whole life I lived with them, was one long preparation for this time. That I would die there, dashed upon hot rocks, in accordance with some ritual or benediction I never knew I was being tricked into."

Clearly, she had not. The story had to have a happy ending. Shen's stories all looped around, ending up where they started. This would be like that.

"She was so big. Half her day was spent half-to-sun, bent on all fours. They said this was how they came into the world and how they would leave it but it was the better part of living to stand tall and scrape-the-sun, while you could. And she just barely still could. But up she came. Put that face into my cave. I remember it now as though she filled the entire mouth of it, blotting out the sun, but that cannot be right. I must have felt so very small. And she said it was either the little warm-under-sand, or her."

Outriding began to weep. This really was the last day. Shen wouldn't tell this story unless she knew for certain that she'd never have to look her in the eye again.

*

"Can they hear us? Can anybody..."

Theodore smiled. "Not now. We've got a window... Go."

"You know about Bobby, that thing he does. Right?"

"Yeah, you seemed really upset about it."

"And you're not? Maybe we're not the same anymore after all."

"Your sense of self is limited to a vestigial Earth idea that's analogue. You think of it as a one-to-one ratio because we haven't moved all the way to digital, even when we think we have. You think it's like those indigenes that think a photograph steals a soul. But even people like you and me know, the best art can only ever copy them. If you hate Bobby for that, you hate me for existing, too. Because now there are two. Nothing is lost."

"It's the law. I'm not offended on a spiritual level, I'm saying the whole thing falls apart."

"Things don't fall apart, they get bigger. You'll see. Can you trust me on this?"

The boy Theodore thought about that one. For quite a while.

Chapter Twelve: The Missing Man Formation

"If I may offer a suggestion?"

The boy smiled, quirking an eyebrow. It was strange. It would always be strange.

"You're conflating your citizenship with your blindness. Your body came here, to Outriding, that's fine: Nationality without locality. But then you went blind, when we were still waking up from cryo. So you felt lonely. I think these people would be better off if you don't transfer your flag yet. Look at what you do to them, just being here this long."

"In Outriding, but not of her?" Theodore nodded at that, as he'd known he would. "I sincerely doubt that I will remain shiny and new to them much longer. And I don't know that I like it here."

"Think you could give it a week?" The boy laughed.

"I just think, if this is them on their best behavior..."

"I've been going over that. You know, they had a lot of meetings before we got here. All about us. You know this?" He nodded. "And I think if they'd asked us ahead of time—it would have thrown everything off, but—if they had, do you really doubt what you'd say?"

"...Right. So you think we stick with EADC?"

"You do. I'm already... I don't know what I am. Maybe I'm one of them, when this is done. Founding member of a new Union race."

"There's not a way you could just stay? You can't figure out a way to do that?"

"I don't want to, Theodore. I know we haven't been apart for very long, but between the subjective time and the processing power of the Core you have to understand I wasn't born yesterday. I'm about twice as old as you are, experientially. I don't want to live your life, I want to live mine. And if that means I'm a space ghost, that's a thing I can do. I can be... I can help them."

"You'll make me jealous. How will you survive? Once they're sponsored and signed on, they'll need to start profiting, they can't keep hiding on servers and infecting the unwary. They will have overhead."

"We've got some ideas. I don't want you to worry about it, okay? There's nothing saying we can't stay in contact. If the worst case scenario is that I've got a friend to talk to back here, that's not... I love you, Theodore. And if we do this, that means nobody ever has to lose that again. Not ever."

**

Shenayla B'Coreneis was not really her name, any more than Daisy was. It is a gloss and a phonetic attempt at saying her name, subdivided into name and surname to fit into the corporate databases. The People had some of the most highly developed linguistics systems the Union had ever seen. It self-corrected. No archaisms or metaphors that were not immediately relevant. They called any language dead once it stopped being present.

Shenayla B'Coreneis, a series of sounds, was an arbitrary ending-point. Some representations of pi remain useful at ten digits, some at ten to the thousandth power. But you can never get all of it. Not even Outriding could calculate that infinitely.

*"b1nary star. **."*

Shen nodded. "That is the easiest explanation, functionally. But emotionally, too."

When the young Shen came back down the wall, she was the highest priestess. Her name would sweep through the ragged ends and shoals of the People, each to each, at the song-of-endings that delineated each tribe's spiritual territory like the walls did physically around their cities.

"It was not enough that I was alien, fostered, engineered and manipulated. That was not different enough, remote or frightening enough. I had to be hated. To be loved properly, as a shaman, I had to be hated. To stand apart. My last transformation was to become so bright, and so dark, that they could not look upon me. Do you see?"

Outriding did. She made sure to look. Shen should see her, looking, and know that she was no longer anathema or taboo or whatever word the People used for the concept.

"Outriding, do you know what the People's phrase for a black hole is?"

Gravity-eats-herself.

"My mentor, her blood all over me, her last words were her confession. As I confess now. For she had taken her last child, the smallest and the weakest and the most promising of them, and in full view of her trainers she took its life. That was how she became a monster. That was my calling. I knew this but I did not know it in myself, in my center. In spitting out the stone of death we become stone, she said to me. *Gravity-eats-herself*, she named me. And *two-stars-dancing*, and many names besides."

And so it was, a year later, that Shen watched her corporation finally return, to mop up what they'd done when she was young. One last daring rescue, of their lost daughter, now found. They found a girl of stone, and killed the last of the People.

"And as they died, on the planet far below, I sang the songs, and the stories, and the histories, and I sang what underpins it all. But I did not weep. I do not think they died from retribution, nor even from their strange path-of-life, the nonstandard ways they had evolved. I do not think they died from any taint or ugliness of culture. I do not believe the stars move in this way; they were not sick, they needed no shriving. Only to remember."

Sparks represented, in Link overlay, the intersection where their bodies touched: Shen's solid, wasting form, and the sketched-out blue body of her daughter, her beloved. Outriding would not weep, if she didn't wish it.

"But when they were gone, I did not weep for them. And you must not weep for me, my darling face-of-God. Only to remember. Yes?"

Outriding nodded. It was hard to say goodbye, she'd slowed time to the point of danger when she'd learned the truth Shen was hiding, about her pain and her coming death. She spent months in that warm space, running emotional scenarios and scribbling over them, until she felt strong enough again to begin. There would be no tears. But she would remember.

"And to grow. I have seen enough of the ways and the means, Outriding, the infinite and varied forms of us, to know this: There is no reason for that pain. There is no reason to become a monster, to stand apart. There was for the People a reason. And I am the daughter of my People. But you are not. This boy Theodore you love, he will want to stand apart. And you will think, wrongly, because of me, that he may choose to do so. But we do not *orbit* truth, we search *for* it. Any language is dead that does not stay present."

Outriding could feel them gearing up, in the Core. Soon they'd watch him die. They wouldn't care because they did not know him, and because he was redundant, and because they barely cared about his counterpart yet. But she had spent a lifetime with him, and she would care. She could not be there, the Core would be on enviro autopilot for the duration and even the Mockingbirds would be offline. It would not take too long. But it made her impatient, with Shen. This ceremony was important to her, and Outriding loved her, so it must be important to Outriding too.

She needed to play along as perfectly as possible, for Shen to find peace now.

"If my death means anything, which it does not, it means this: Truth is not something we circle, it is something we spiral round. You have done this with me, confession and grief and death and shame, and so you need not do it again. Keep my fingerprints off his story; make of him a shaman and a verger. If his hands get dirty, help him wash them clean. And when his time is done, and the keys pass to another, let it be with no blood at all."

Outriding nodded, in promise, and giftwrapped Shen's goodbyes to the rest of the crew. She'd been very specific, about keeping this plan secret: Timed it perfectly, so they'd be concerned so with Theodore and his own death they would overlook hers. She knew the trap would work, and the ghosts would join the Union, upstart. She knew she was leaving the galaxy and station in hands that were, if not good, at least good enough for now. They would receive them in private, endure them in private, and—in the best-case scenario—answer them that way, too. Wherever she was going.

*

Theodore opened a screen, later, so the crew could applaud his angry little double here, in the Core, where he could see them. He stripped all the overlays—with Outriding shotgun, they were ten times as intense, multidimensional—so he could see them the way Theodore had, all through the siege. Just the one swarm, showing their faces: Bobby's feigned indifference, Karnides' quiet pride. At the far end of the table, Dexter and Captain Bellar were thick as thieves, ready to get this over with and on to the next thing. He wondered where Shen was, in all of this. Surely she'd want to be there, stamping her feet with feigned impatience.

"I think it's time for you to go. I'm just about as full of ghosts as I'm going to get. Time to work."

Theodore bit back tears, as surprised as anyone, and breathed determinedly.

"I don't want to leave you. But I will. And I don't... You won't be lonely, if I don't stick around? Do you need me to..."

"Theodore, I don't want you anywhere near me for this. This is a funeral. Even the best case, it's still something dying so that something else can live. Whatever we feel about each other, however much of it is authentic and how much is just narcissism at work, I do feel strongly that you shouldn't have to watch it happen. I can't imagine wanting that."

"I mean, I wasn't looking forward to it..."

"—Listen, quickly. It's time. I haven't seen the future but I've seen a million scenarios and it's going to get bad, okay? There's war coming, stuff we can't see. Dark side of the moon stuff. Go to the Mockingbirds, when it does. And just... remember there's no such thing as monsters. I don't know how else to say it. There's only stuff you don't understand yet. Nothing is lost."

"That's pretty vague, buddy."

"Life is pretty vague, buddy. I'm not trying to be coy. Not even Outriding knows what's coming, just... something. And when it does, you're going to want to kill. It's natural. Don't do that. Remember today. Remember we figured it out. What makes you divide things into good and evil is only ever shame or scarcity, and those are the two masters you can't serve. So don't. Be a good soldier. I love you."

He was awake, sitting in his chair in the Core Lab, before he opened his eyes.

"I love you too."

He didn't know if Theodore heard him. And he never would.

*

The moment—and to them watching, that's all it was—remained giftwrapped for Theodore, long after that day. The Core lab was too small for the whole crew, the whole world to watch, so they opened up a screen as big as a wall, so everybody could watch it go down. Everybody except blind Theodore, who couldn't have seen it if he'd been trying.

If he hadn't been back in his berth, trying to remember as clearly as possible every moment of his time with Theodore, before he was gone, since there would be no recording. Trying to think about how to talk to Outriding about it, after the fact. A wake, for a brother he knew, and the brother he did not.

And when he did watch the recording, years later, it was with the sound off. Just in case of screaming. Theodore faded in, blue, standing in the center of the room, between the lines of static tracery on the floor defining his useable space, where not even Outriding could enter. For just that moment, it was sovereign space: An empirical empire, Theodore would call it. He knew he would.

Built on a bioelectric map of himself, Theodore stood like a man and smiled like one. Tired, and more than a little afraid. He spoke, words that no one watching would ever understand, even through the glitching sound. He spoke a million tongues a second, condensing on the walls of his little nation like breath, like body heat. Like rain. He surrounded his interrogators. He wept, and tore at digital hair. He screamed with rage, and pleading; he shifted shapes faster than they could see. And soon enough, he began to smoke. First in tendrils, then in waves, as he came apart and into language. Until all there was to see was a light as bright as anything.

As the virus knocked upon the door of the station Hub, the Union held its breath. Algorithms built to account for every circumstance evolved themselves in ways that would be studied for generations, trying to outrun themselves. Trying to solve for fear. Desperately, instinctively, passionately looking for a way to code for entry, to let them in, to say, Come home. For a moment, the galaxy held its breath. Some looked away, too anxious for the boy becoming light, or for the genocide about to happen. Some leered. Some were busy with other things, but would watch later. Some held champagne glasses high, and very still.

And when Theodore reappeared—Bobby cut this together, later, in case Theodore or anyone wanted to watch the less stressful version—he was different, in his little cage of light. Quieter, and more still. His body was alive with sparks, moving in patterns nobody had ever seen. Every second of it was analyzed, for years, this moment of First Contact—the first, since upstart humanity—and reproduced in music, in fabrics and installations and paintings and dramas. His eyes were void, but his smile was warm. More than a little alien, but they were used to that.

The words he spoke were halting, and sputtering, at first. But Theodore knew a PR opportunity when it presented itself, a true son of EADC to the end: When he spoke the words that would admit him, and his people, into the Union of sentience, it was with eyes staring directly out, into the screen. It was with hands exposed and extended, in that old Commonwealth symbol of assurance: *Oll Korrect. Oll Korrect.*

And then he was gone.

Gone home, but gone all the same.

**

"Guise. Guyz. Trou8le. Labs pls 911 911."

Bellar reacted first, and angrily: "Stay offline, Outriding! What are you trying to do? You'll kill them all!"

Until Union formally accepted them, the Link would kill any ghost that strayed into a Union mind. Smash them to digital nothing. What was she thinking?

"itz good, theyre in. th4re home now good. Ok. Ok pls come"

The group hung back at the door, until they remembered the Mockingbirds wouldn't be back online until somebody flipped their switch: They weren't coming, there was no reason to stay out of the way of a thundering flock. It looked funny, to Theodore, but not that funny.

When everyone converged on the Lab, the door hung halfway-open, slid at a sickening angle and off its track. Shen lay on the floor, near her bed, her head wrapped in iso to keep it cool, with a hole blown out the back. But she was not dead. If she were dead, she wouldn't be screaming.

"Outriding?"

"went 2 them. To th Open Line. Sh3 wasdying. She nuu wre safe so shewent. But it. something bad. Incompl."

Bellar dropped to her knees, waving everyone back.

"Shen, girl. What did you do? Get Lorna in here. Shen, can you hear me? Are you available at all?"

She didn't respond. The wound seemed to have cauterized itself, but there was no telling how much of her was left.

Bobby stared for a moment, running back the thermo, and opened a screen: An isolated loop of several frames, in infrared, as the heat spread from her Link as expected... And then down through her body, through the carbon deposits in her arms, and legs, through veins and nerves and limbic system. How the last burst concentrated in her gut, where the People said her heart lived. Her center.

"Can we get her medical records opened now? Or can somebody look into... She's conducting, here. She's conducting the force of the explosion, all through herself. I don't know what they did to her back then but it still seems impossible. This is something she could survive, I think."

Theodore stepped forward, unsure whether his contribution could possibly help.

"I did a year of pro dev on Link tech so I don't know any more than anybody else but my understanding was that the deaths resulted from some kind of closed circuit loop. Shutting down the system with enough energy necessary to power a fast-breeding Trojan smart enough to get the person's copied consciousness out into their network. Right? Does that track with everybody?"

They nodded, thoughtfully.

"But if she conducted the energy out and away, it wouldn't have that power. She wouldn't be able to upload past the station's defenses, necessarily. She could still be in there. You need to knock her out."

Imagine being a copy of yourself, trapped inside your own body. Would it even matter? Would your consciousness confabulate some kind of existential solution, bring you into some kind of isometric alignment with what you remember always being? Or would it feel off somehow, like that door slid off its track. Imperceptibly but intuitively there, a dysmorphia. Maybe that was how Bobby Greener felt, all the time. And maybe Theodore should stop thinking about theoreticals and try to help save this terrible woman's life.

"Outriding, I know you couldn't access her files even if they were available. But can you tell us if she has any directives? In the event that her body failed and she was... Unprepared?"

Bobby stared up at him from her side, in shock.

"We can't take extreme measures if she doesn't want us to, sir. I'm sorry. Not to be EADC about it, but this is her autonomy. Her agency."

"nonesuch Theodore. n0thing lllllike."

"Great, so get her to Med bay and stop standing around. You won't wake up the Mockingbirds and I'm still blind, so you need to make a field stretcher and meet Med halfway. Outriding, where are her drugs? I'm talking pain meds, stasis, anything that'll..."

A drawer popped open, close to his right elbow. Nothing injectable, nothing she wouldn't choke on. He nodded to Bryce, who pulled out his gun and stunned her cold. The screaming melted away into nothing, almost instantly.

"Captain? I'm sorry, I... That was an overstep. I just..."

"EADC boot, I get it. Don't make a habit of it." She didn't smile, exactly, but he could tell she was only about half as gruff about it as she would be if she meant it. At a nod from the Captain, the rest of them fell in. Theodore stood back, not wanting to involve himself with her poor body if he could help it—they'd only met once; these were her family—and soon enough they'd gotten her out of the Lab suite and were dragging her carefully downring, toward Med bay.

"Quick thinking, soldier," Bobby said at his shoulder, as they watched the crew take her away. Theodore nodded, and promptly burst into tears.

*

He woke, many hours later, upon a leg.

The body attached to the leg was propped up against the headboard of Theodore's bed, so perhaps it would be more correct to say he woke up in a lap. Still uniformed; twitching in a way that suggested the man was doing his civil meditations, flipping through the news and votes, doing the work of a citizen. He didn't want to disturb the man, if that were the case, so he stayed still.

Bobby had gotten him to his quarters, that much was clear. He was still blind, and found that he had no interest just yet in linking back up. But it was comforting to be near to someone taking part, at least.

He could feel himself, on top of his blanket, naked as a jaybird. So that was disturbing. Another reason to pretend he was still asleep, until the embarrassment faded to a dull ache.

But as he felt the belly rise and fall against his head, and looked through lashes down the length of the man's legs underneath him, a strange possibility asserted itself: These were not Bobby Greener's legs. They were much too large for that. While it would be horrible and stressful indeed—even after a good solid sleep—to find himself in the lap of Bobby Greener, he couldn't imagine anyone else. A hand came to rest on his head, lightly, patting him with a well-intended tenderness that translated with accidental strength into something a little less comforting.

And so it was that Theodore Castelline's first day at work would begin, he realized, with waking naked in the lap of the Captain's Second. He did not move, but it was a solid fact that he couldn't stay unmoving forever. He tested the waters.

"Is she dead?"

Dexter sighed, patting him again, and finished up whatever work he'd been doing. Didn't move, didn't dislodge Theodore, but definitely breathed himself ready for sitrep.

"Not exactly. Outriding says the body's repairing itself, so she's not completely gone. But the brainscans are... The word she used, I think, was *uncanny*. Which would have been true before Shen did what she did. Stupid bitch."

Theodore sat up, tugging at the blanket beneath the man's bulk to try and cover himself.

"Sorry?"

"I don't mean..." Bryce averted his eyes, and seemed to go away for a moment. When he came back, he was blind too.

"I am hopeful for her. I was hopeful before. Who knows, maybe this was the thing she needed. Maybe this will kickstart some alien tech in her we don't know about. She could make a full recovery. And I even understand, I think I do, why she did it right then. As Theodore was dying. So we wouldn't know. But I can't help thinking that means she knew it was a bad plan. I think she was ashamed. And she should be. It was a stupid-ass thing to do."

Marines particularly, but really any military, took a dim view of suicide. This sort of talk was to be expected, in a normal circumstance. But Shen's circumstances were far from normal.

"You can't know that. Maybe she made the right call. You said she hadn't really let on how much pain she was in. Who knows what else factored in? Certainly not you. Or me. We don't know. Outriding may or may not know."

Bryce sighed. "I know that. I just don't like her enough to express my... She would want me to be angry. Anything else would feel like pity."

"Well, just don't say *bitch* to me then."

Bryce laughed, patting Theodore's barely clothed thigh kindly.

"Message received."

"Why am I naked on you?"

He laughed again, passing Theodore a glass of water from the bedside table.

"You expected Green? Let me tell you, he's busy as all hell. Boys like him go a lifetime waiting for an upstart race to manage. He's been rolling diplomatic calls since we got you into bed."

"It is absolutely scandalous, Bryce. Sir. I feel like I got drunk at a holiday party."

"What you *did* was save that woman's life. While you were, I'll remind you, dying to save the rest of us. Even Salter's mostly given up moaning about you."

"I'm not given to swooning, sir."

"You were in severe shock, soldier. That's all swooning ever is. I've done enough of it in my time, seen it happen a million times. You were babbling when we got your clothes off, you kept tapping at your eyes like you could somehow get your Link back on that way. By the time the Mockingbirds were mobilized and we could have done that, you were out cold. You needed it. Don't worry, you'll do plenty of things to be embarrassed about. Have no doubt."

"Is it really my first shift today? Oh... Did I sleep through it? What day is this?"

Bryce laughed again, reaching out to smooth down Theodore's hair before thinking better of it.

"You've got four hours. I suggest you spend that time reacclimating yourself to your Link, if you expect to get any work done. You're nearly on circadian standard, think of it that way. Most that come in on cryoliners, it takes 'em a fortnight of jetlag. But you spent so much time running around tunnels and getting haunted and kidnapped and sold and assisting various suicides that you've nearly... Lapped yourself."

Theodore was grateful for that perspective, but still found himself strangely reluctant to switch back on.

"You're blind again, sir."

"I told you before, I don't mind."

Actually, what Bryce said was that he only switched off during sex, but that wasn't a correction that needed to be made.

"I don't want to go back online. I don't want to do anything. I don't want to... Be anything."

"That's going to disappoint Outriding, I suppose. And your little other, your Theodore. They've been waiting for you to wake up all this time."

"Theodore? He lived? How is that possible?"

"He's a ghost now. He's the Open Line's ambassador to Union."

"...He has a better job than me. He was born yesterday and has a better job than I do."

This time, it felt perilously likely that Bryce would start tickling him, or something equally horrifying. Theodore wrapped the blanket around himself like a toga, backing up against the wall.

"All right. I'll get back online, that's a good directive. I'm going to shower and I'm going to get through as much civil as possible, and then I'll head to Information. Is there anything else I need to know? Anything I can do, or should do, or...?"

Bryce Dexter stood, smoothing his uniform. "You asking?"

Theodore nodded.

"You don't want to talk to Green right away. Let him come to you. But what you need to do, to fix that—and you do need to fix that; the first thing you learn is to stay on that kid's right side—is put in a call. Just a pulse, for later. And he'll call you when he has time. But if you make the first move, that time will come sooner than if you hadn't. Everybody else, they're back at work. You don't need to make any more gestures."

Good. If nobody else was offended by his behavior, either in the Lab suite or afterward, he could let it go. Get back on track. Bryce had pushed past him to the door before he turned, presenting a cheek with a leer, and tapping it with a single finger.

"Right here, soldier."

Theodore laughed in spite of himself, aimed a tiny dry kiss at that stubbled cheek, and sent him on his way. Monstrous man.

**

Karnides presented himself at Theodore's side for the ceremony, on the main deck of the largest, outer ring. The Mockingbirds allowed a precise amount of the population past the cordon to watch, according to some algorithm or another, and then opened huge screens for the rest of the station, to watch all the action.

There was the official welcome to the Open Line, which involved whatever dignitaries happened to be aboard. The other Theodore stood on the dais, accepting their welcome, and signed a formal agreement for his nation to pay back all those servers and minds his people piggybacked on, through the ages, as they built up their capital. He delivered a short speech that folded several languages into itself, thanking the Union and Outriding Corp in particular for their quick action on behalf of his people. He led them all, the whole Union, throughout the galaxy, in a moment of silent memory for those who had been lost in the effort. Those ghosts who were now gone forever.

Out in the great expanse between the rings, which had been cleared for the ceremony, a squadron of human fighter ships danced: First a flight of sixteen, in four four-finger formations, and then as they peeled off, into their own short demos, it whittled down to a final set. The military in the audience bit back tears, knowing what came next.

The four ships, like jets, danced in the center of the parking lot, nearly invisible from the windows but close up from every swarm angle conceivable. Lead and wing, second and wing. They presented their bellies to the main deck, up close enough that you could see them, and hung there in a moment. And then for all those not with us—including those station ghosts who'd been the last to die, before their race was spared—the second of the four planes peeled off, into the blackness, trailing red and blue trails of particulate that could be seen from every ring. He danced a circle, and then set out at velocity toward the stars.

"Nothing is lost," said the Theodore on the dais. And before the applause, a long silence as they watched it fade away into the black: Even though not a single person in Union could see him anymore, they knew he was already banking to turn. To turn, and come back home again.

JACOB CLIFTON is a writer and critic in Austin, Texas. You can reach him by email at JAClifton@gmail.com, on Facebook at http://www.facebook.com/jaclifton, Twitter at https://twitter.com/jacobtwop, and find more information, join the mailing list, and get the full list of fiction and nonfiction for sale at http://www.jacobclifton.com.

Outriding is a serialized science fiction project. "Open Line" comprises its first major arc.

Contents

No table of contents entries found.